WINTER'S SILENCE

Stephanie Silberstein

Narrow Path Publishing
Fayetteville, North Carolina 2008

Cover art and design by David Chayim
Cover photograph by Shoshannah Stone

This novel is a work of fiction. Names, characters, places and incidents are either the product of the author's imagination, or are used fictitiously. Any resemblance to actual persons, living or dead, or events is entirely coincidental.

Publisher's Cataloging-in-Publication
(Provided by Quality Books, Inc.)

Silberstein, Stephanie.
Winter's silence / Stephanie Silberstein.
p. cm.
LCCN 2008902556
ISBN-13: 978-0-9816459-0-2
ISBN-10: 0-9816459-0-9

1. Jewish children--New York (State)--Fiction.
2. Jewish families--New York (State)--Fiction.
3. Antisemitism--New York (State)--Fiction. 4. New York (State)--Fiction. 5. Domestic fiction. 6. Jewish fiction. 7. Christmas stories, American. I. Title.

PS3619.I5434W56 2008 813'.6
QBI08-600121

This novel is dedicated to my G-d and to the One who came to bring us all closer together in love.

It is also dedicated to the memory of David Newton, who sought a world where everyone could be successful.

ACKNOWLEDGMENTS

My heartfelt thanks go out to my cover artist/designer, David Chayim (http://www.myspace.com/david_artist), and my photographer, Shoshannah Stone. You two are the most supportive people in my life, always ready to tell me how awesome what I'm doing is and to give me constructive criticism when I need it. Thank you for being the best friends in the entire world!

Thank you also to my family for encouraging me to complete and publish *Winter's Silence:* my mother, father, and sister for being my first readers, my brother for being my first and fairest reviewer, and my extended family for their excitement and encouragement.

Finally, a sincere thanks to my Bladen Lakes "family", especially those of you who eagerly awaited the book's publication. It goes without saying that you are way superior to the teachers and administrators in this novel and I am honored to share my success with you.

ONE

Everything was all slushy on the way home from school. I tiptoed carefully round the puddles, Leigh steered her bike right through them. The wind messed up her braids, yellow hair went in her mouth and over her eyes like it was snow.

I wished I had a bike too. I covered the note pinned to my jacket and prayed that Mama would use her soft voice on me when she read it.

Leigh hummed a Christmas song as we rounded the corner. "I can't wait 'til the concert, can you, Emily?"

I shrugged.

"C'mon," Leigh said. "It'll be so fun."

I scraped melting snow off my boot. "But there's no Jewish stuff."

"There's a menorah next to the tree, isn't there?"

I pushed my hands down deep into my pockets, I wanted to fold myself up. "Yeah, but . . ."

Something hit the back of my head and slid down my neck to under my shirt. A slushball.

I turned just in time to see dumb, fat Joey laughing. "Gotcha," he said, and in a quiet voice he added something that sounded like, "Jew."

My eyes burned me. A car honked, Leigh grabbed my arm. I looked both ways and ran across the street. I got across safe but there was ice on the sidewalk, I slipped and slid towards my house. I got up and flipped my zipper up and down 'til my eyes stopped wanting to cry.

Leigh's bike crashed down. "Don't—"

"I'm fine." I reached under my shirt for the key I wished was round my neck like Leigh has round hers. My hands burned with cold. I marched to the front door and rang the doorbell.

No one answered.

I twisted my elbow around to look at the scar where I fell and rang the bell again. A big family of birds flew across the sky. They honked loud. I pushed the doorbell all the way in and held it down.

Mama opened the door. Her eyes were wide and blue as lakes and she had her smile on, but her lips were thin. I stared at her while I ripped the note off the pin and came in.

Uncle Max, who was standing behind Mama, pushed the door closed. It squeaked all the way.

The room felt like it was shrinking, Uncle Max looked taller than ever. I held the note out in front of me and took baby steps. "Here, Mama. Miss James said you have to sign this."

"Wipe your boots, please, Emily," Mama said.

I pulled my boots off and put them on the mat. "It wasn't my fault. In music class . . ."

Mama took the note and looked at it but her eyes didn't move. "Uh huh." She walked away.

I pretended I was going upstairs but really I leaned on the banister. I put my hair over my eyes and watched Mama talk to Uncle Max through a red-brown curtain. Uncle Max said something about Alex. Mama said, "The doctor . . ."

I pushed my hair out of my eyes. "What's wrong with Alex?"

Everyone turned and looked at me. Mama's face trembled and I listened for Alex crying but he didn't.

Please God, make Alex OK. I'll be good.

"Nothing's wrong, kiddo," Uncle Max said. I opened my eyes and saw everything was the same except Uncle Max was looking at me. "Alex is just . . . different. His mind is—"

Mama poked Uncle Max with her elbow hard enough to hurt. He didn't flinch. "I think Emily has a right to know what's going on," he said to her.

Mama pushed her teeth together. "I'll tell her in my own way, thank you."

Outside the wind pushed a tree branch against the window. I couldn't stop shivering, I sat down and hugged myself.

Uncle Max looked at me. I pretended I was a snowflake melting into the stairs but he didn't look away.

"It wasn't my fault," I said. "Miss James—"

"Look, Emily . . ."

"Maxwell," Mama said. "Come help me with dinner." Mama's eyes were big and round and on fire. Uncle Max's head drooped as he followed her.

The kitchen door squeaked closed. I pushed myself up the steps with my hands even though Mama always tells me not to. I waited at the top but the grown-ups stayed in the kitchen.

I lay flat on my belly and crawled like a snake into Alex's room. Alex's mobile went round and round. I turned into a big six-year-old girl again and did a push up to get standing up.

Alex was sitting straight up in the crib, there was so much space around him that he looked little even though Daddy says he's big for his age. He was staring at the mobile like it turned him into a statue, he didn't even move when I came in.

I grabbed onto the crib. Alex said, "No," then he switched to baby language and said a bunch of stuff I couldn't understand. He rocked back and forth and shrieked.

I dropped onto my sore knees and squeezed the little bars that held the crib up. I was in jail and Alex was visiting me. I looked at him through the bars. Soft footsteps came down the hall—Uncle Max was coming to visit me too. Mama's footsteps are always loud and the house shakes when she comes up the steps.

Uncle Max leaned against the doorway, watching me. I got up but I stayed behind the crib. "I didn't mean to make Alex cry."

Uncle Max put his hand out like he was gonna ruffle Alex's hair but he just left it hanging. "Don't worry about it. That's just him trying to say something. See, Alex doesn't talk the same way everyone else does. The doctor called it 'autism' but—"

"Emily," Mama called. "Come set the table."

Uncle Max blinked. "Better get downstairs, kiddo."

"I can't. I'm in jail."

Uncle Max patted my hand. "I just let you out. Scoot."

I walked backwards out of the room, watching him.

After Uncle Max went home, Mama put on the radio and put the sweet potatoes in the microwave. I went in front of the radio to block the waves.

Mama said, "Ssh!" and turned the radio up so the waves went through me like Cupid's arrows. The traffic report was on. Mama stood frozen like when you hit "pause" on the VCR.

I looked out the window. Snow melted off a big tree and went drip, drip, drip into the driveway. Everything looked ugly and slushy and naked. I squeezed my tummy. "Mama, I'm starving."

Mama turned on the sink and scrubbed a pot. "Go see if your brother's up from his nap."

I backwards-walked to the kitchen door but I didn't go any further. Instead I watched Mama scrub the pot. A big boy coasted down the street on his bike, I saw him from the window. The front door squeaked as he went away.

I took my note off the kitchen table and backwards-walked to the living room. Daddy almost bumped me on his way in. "Hi, sweetie," he said, peeling off his gloves.

I followed Daddy back into the kitchen. "Miss James gave me this note cause—"

"Traffic's insane. And this weather." Daddy shoved his gloves into his pockets. "We about ready to do candles?"

Mama's back stiffened, but she nodded. I followed Daddy into the dining room. "Daddy, my note."

Daddy pushed two candles into the menorah. "You know what, Emily? This year you're big enough to do this with me." He lit a match. The flame was blue and yellow and it looked mad. I stared into it, the note fell out of my hands.

Daddy lit the top candle. I wondered what the flame would do if I poked it. Daddy grabbed my wrist. His mouth opened and closed like a fish that couldn't breathe right. "Don't . . . here, do it with me." He guided my wrist towards the candle bottom. He pulled so hard it hurt.

"Daddy?" I said, but he was already singing in Hebrew.

I picked up the note and went on the other side of the menorah, behind the candles. I read aloud while Daddy finished singing the prayer. Maybe the words would bump each other in the air and get to everybody's ears. "Dear Dr. and Mrs. Horowitz: It is with regret that I must tell you that Emily was not behaving in music class today. While the other students—"

The kitchen door swung open. Mama stood in the doorway. From behind the candles she looked like a shadowy ghost. I stopped reading. Daddy looked at me, then back at the candles.

"Mama?" I said. Mama didn't answer. I looked back and forth from Mama to Daddy to the candles. Fire-spots danced in front of me. I rubbed my eyes but the spots didn't go away.

"Dinner's ready," Mama said. Daddy went to go get Alex.

I slid the note across to Mama before I kicked out my chair. She picked it up and folded and unfolded it. It looked like a little bird that wanted to fly away.

"About that note," I said. I pushed my hand into the chair 'til it left a mark. "Uhm . . . what happened was, Miss James wanted us to sing Christmas songs." I waited for Mama and Daddy to look shocked but they didn't. "Songs to *Jesus*." I slapped my hand over my mouth to push the name back in.

Daddy tossed a spoonful of potatoes onto his plate. "Always listen to your teacher."

"But Daddy, it's wrong. We don't—"

Mama put the note down. "Eat your dinner, Emily. I'll sign this in the morning. I let go of the chair top, she leaned over me and said to Daddy, "Alex had his appointment this afternoon."

Daddy spooned potatoes onto my plate. I stirred them with my fork to keep the butter from melting into them and making them sick.

Mama put her hand on my wrist and went on talking to Daddy. I turned towards the menorah and looked at the two candles burning. "Does God live inside the flame?"

Mama and Daddy stopped their conversation. "God is everywhere," Mama said. She turned back to Daddy. "Anyway, Maxwell thinks I'm overreacting but it just seems like a damn serious diagnosis."

I turned away from the flame again, just in case, and started to cross myself the way Leigh does when she gets upset. Expect in the middle I bumped my hands together and pretended I was just squeezing them.

Mama looked at me. "What are you doing, Emily?"

I shoved my hands in my pockets. "Nothing." Mama went on looking at me. I slid down in my seat to hide from her eyes.

"Straighten up, Emily," Daddy said. I sat up in my seat again but I put my hand over my eyes so the candles couldn't see inside me.

After a long time Daddy slammed his spoon down. He reached over and pushed my fork into my hand. "Stop the nonsense," he said. His lips were thin and pressed together, his words came out by magic.

I took a bite of potato. It burned my mouth.

Daddy turned away from me. He and Mama went on talking.

The candles went on burning.

Outside the melting snow went drip drip drip against the window.

I slid down in my seat again. Under the table I crossed myself for real and hoped God understood.

TWO

I couldn't feel my feet underneath the cold when I woke up the next morning. I pulled my pajama socks all the way up and wrapped my feet tight in the blanket but the cold still got in anyway. I put the blanket all the way over me and lay flat and listened. I was a soldier in the middle of a war and the enemy was close by.

I couldn't hear anything.

My door squeaked open. I watched Mama from under the blanket. Her eyes were big and black and droopy. She was holding Alex, his head was droopy too. The rest of him was all stiff.

Mama rocked Alex. "Emily."

I crawled out from under the blanket. "Is Alex over his autism yet?"

"You're awake. Good." Mama pulled on the rope to open my curtains. Light came in the room, it threw a shadow down on the carpet. "Hurry up and get dressed."

I got out of bed and stuck my foot in the sun shadow to warm it up.

"I mean it," Mama said. "Don't dawdle." She held Alex close against her and left the room.

Mama was talking to Alex in baby language all the way down the hall. I dropped to my knees and crawled across to the dresser. If I turned into a baby, would I understand baby language too? I listened hard but all I could hear was Mama's footsteps going thump, thump, thump down the steps.

After I got dressed, I ran down the hall and slid down the steps to save time. Mama saw me sliding as she went into the kitchen. She kept going.

I ran after her.

There was a little package of oatmeal sitting on my napkin. I picked it up and read the back.

"There's hot water on the stove," Mama said. Alex traced the lines on his tray with his finger. Mama grabbed his wrist. "Don't burn yourself."

I stared out the window while I opened the oatmeal. Water dripped off the roof onto the car top. In the abandoned house next door, the wind blew the ivy back and forth.

I shivered and went in the dining room.

The flames were gone, the candles were all melted into little pieces of junk in the bottom of the menorah. A match was lying on the table. It was black and dead too.

I picked up my note and stuffed it into my pocket.

I went back in the kitchen. "I'm cold."

Mama didn't answer. She was talking to Alex again.

I opened up the note and read it inside my head while I waited. When I came to the end, God pulled my head up high.

The note was not signed.

Cold came in through the window and sank into my tummy. I squeezed the note. "Mama?"

Mama pushed a spoon into Alex's hand and held his wrist down. He whimpered and tried to get away. "Go get ready," Mama said. "You don't want to keep Leigh waiting."

"Mama, my note."

Alex rocked back and forth and made the high chair shake. He pushed his bowl away with his head. I giggled. Mama looked up and I slapped my hand over my mouth to push the giggle back in.

Alex hit the bowl with his head over and over and over. Mama tried to push the bowl away. He smashed his head against her hand. She let him go and stood squeezing her wrist. Then she took his napkin and dabbed at the spilled oatmeal on his tray.

I took a step back. Mama looked at me but she went on washing the tray. I stuffed the note into my pocket again and turned and walked away, I held my head high like a grown-up's.

In the front hall, I put on my outside things in a big hurry. I was a spy going on a secret mission and if I didn't leave now, the country was in trouble.

I pulled at the front door. It was hard to open with gloves on, but I squeezed my eyes shut and pulled with all my might. The door squeaked open. I looked over my shoulder. The coast was clear. I tiptoed outside and shut the door behind me.

The snow was all melted away even though it was still very cold. I walked as fast as I could without making any noise. Leigh came down the sidewalk behind me. I could hear her shoelaces going clack clack clack. "Emily!" she called.

I turned and put my finger on my lips. "We don't want the enemy to get us."

Leigh ran towards me anyway. "Guess what? Someone's moving into the abandoned house. My mom said."

I tiptoed down the sidewalk. Leigh kept running. I crouched down 'til I was almost crawling and ducked into the bushes in front of the big house at the end of the block.

Leigh joined me. "What are you doing?"

"I'm a spy, so I gotta stay in hiding." I took the note out of my pocket. "You take this, just in case."

Leigh looked at the note but she didn't take it. She wrinkled up her forehead and put her finger on each word. After a long time, she looked up. "It's not signed."

I stared at my boots. They were wet and shiny and I could see a little bit of my face in them.

"Don't worry," Leigh said. "Here." She pulled the note out of my hand. I thought maybe it would rip into five million billion pieces and then it would be like Miss James never wrote it. But my gloves were slippery and the note fell out of them without anything happening to it.

I watched in my boots as Leigh scribbled on the bottom of the note. She gave it back to me. "Let's go so we're not late."

I stuffed the note down deep in my pocket and hoped Miss James would forget to ask about it.

The floor in the school was shiny and slippery like an ice skating rink. I shuffled and slid all the way to the little room at the end of the hall. Everybody was talking at the same time while they put their coats away in their cubbies. I put my hands over my ears and watched them.

Miss James was at her desk reading something, her long black hair made shadows on the page so I couldn't see. She looked up. Her smile was full of white teeth like the Big Bad Wolf. "Come on in, Emily," she said.

I was still ice skating, I took baby steps into the room so I wouldn't fall down.

"I moved the seats around," Miss James said. "You're over here now." She led me to a desk and chair underneath a big snowflake. I kept my eye on the snowflake while I got in the chair. Then I looked down.

Joey was sitting across from me, leaning his chair back so far he was almost falling over.

I opened my desk and pretended to be looking for something.

"Oh, by the way, Emily," Miss James said, "did you get your note signed for me?"

I pulled my head up out of the desk. Joey was grinning. I dug in my pocket for the note but I kept my eyes locked on Joey like photon torpedoes. I handed it to Miss James without moving out of range.

The last bell rang. Miss James made us stand up and say the Pledge of Allegiance. Then she sat down at the piano and played *My Country 'Tis of Thee.* I knew all the words but I pretended to be stupid, I just hummed them. Miss James didn't notice.

When the bell rang at the end of math time, Miss James stood up and took a little step towards me. Her dress was wrinkled. She smoothed it so no one would laugh at her.

The bell rang again. "Playground time," Miss James said. She smiled but the smile faded away.

Everyone ran to their cubbies at once, they pushed and shoved and made a lot of noise. I put my math notebook away in my desk and sat and watched them.

Miss James turned into an elephant herder and got everybody out. She didn't see me 'til she was finished. Then she stood looking at me. "Why, Emily," she said, "don't you want to go play?"

I shrugged.

Miss James walked over to the window and looked out. "It is a little cold for playing outside," she said. "But you can't sit in here. The playground teacher is expecting you."

I pulled my coat off my chair and shoved my arms into the sleeves. My gloves fell out onto the floor.

"Here," Miss James said. "Let me help you." She picked up the gloves and handed them to me. "There you go. Hurry so you won't be marked absent."

I marched to the door.

"By the way, Emily," Miss James said, "did your mom really sign that note?"

I turned slowly and x-rayed her. Miss James made her eyes wide as lakes and put on her smile face. My insides felt tight. I nodded.

Miss James shuffled the papers on her desk. "Run out to the playground, then."

I shoved my hands into my pockets and turned around, but I didn't run. I took stiff robot steps.

At lunch, me and Leigh sat together at a little table in the corner of the cafeteria. The boys were sitting at a big table, they were banging it and running around and making a lot of noise. I tucked my hair under my hat to make it short while I watched them. Now I was a boy too.

Leigh coughed without covering her mouth. "I hope the new people moving in have a girl our age, don't you?"

I waved Leigh's germs away from my face and took a sip from my juice box. At the boys' table, Joey threw half an apple across the room. It landed right in the middle of the trash.

"He-llo?" Leigh said.

I turned around like I was still a girl. "I guess."

"Well, we have to have another girl." Leigh unwrapped a cookie. "Too many boys make girls dumb. My mom said."

I reached for the cookie without taking my eyes away from Joey. I had to watch him so he wouldn't put a bad magic spell on me. Leigh broke a little piece off and gave it to me.

The loudspeaker crackled. "Emily Horowitz to the principal's office, please."

The whole first grade stopped.

"Ooh," Joey said. "Emily's in trouble."

I jumped up. "Am not."

"Oh, ignore him." Leigh broke off another piece of cookie. "Want me to walk with you?"

I shook my head. Leigh got up anyway. She pushed the cookie piece into my hand. I took it but I didn't do anything with it, I just held it while I walked away.

I marched down the hall without bending my knees, I was a robot soldier going to a trial. When I got to the principal's office I pulled the door open and walked in like the hero in a war movie.

Miss Green looked up from her computer. She smiled at me. Her back teeth were all crooked and I didn't like to look at them. "Oh, there you are, Emily. Have a seat. I'll tell Mr. O'Leary you're here."

Miss Green wrote something in a big notebook. She took a pile of papers off the printer into the back room. The door closed behind her. I listened hard, but I couldn't hear what she was saying to Mr. O'Leary.

The clock on the wall ticked loud. I watched the second hand go around and around. After a long time, the door scratched against the floor and Miss Green came out again. "Here you go, Emily," she said, and tossed a piece of paper onto her desk.

I picked up the piece of paper. The edges were all raggy, it looked like it was torn away from something else. "What's this?"

Miss Green didn't look away from her screen. "Bring that to your mom."

Mr. O'Leary came out of his office while I read the paper. I saw him in the side of my eye.

"This is the same as yesterday," I said.

Mr. O'Leary's underwears were showing. He pulled his pants up. "Well, yes," he said, and took two giant steps so he stood behind Miss Green. "We couldn't quite make out the signature, so just have your mom sign this one and then we can be all done with this." He smiled a big-toothed smile that stayed on his face after it should have been gone already. I looked at a dust rainbow in front of the door so he would stop staring.

Mr. O'Leary cleared his throat. "Miss Green, perhaps you can make sure that Emily doesn't lose that note."

"Of course. Come here, Emily."

Mr. O'Leary went back into his office and closed the door. I watched Miss Green pin the note to my coat pocket to make sure she didn't hurt herself. "There you go," she said, and smiled at me. I told my mouth not to smile back but it didn't listen.

The bell rang.

"Run along now," Miss Green said.

I looked at the ground all the way back to class so I wouldn't step on any hidden land mines.

THREE

It was snowing again by afternoon. Miss James read out loud about a mouse who was friends with a lion while me and Leigh looked out the window. At first it was only snowing a little and melting away as soon as it hit the ground. But then the wind got mad and shook the trees. The snow came down harder and turned the grass white.

Miss James turned a page hard as a big gust of wind threw snow off the trees. "Eyes forward, Emily." I turned around slowly and waited. Miss James didn't say anything to Leigh.

The bell rang. Everybody jumped up and ran to their cubbies. I kept my eye on the window so the snow couldn't melt away while I wasn't looking. I could feel Miss James' eyes on my back, they were burning two little holes like cigarette burns. I turned around.

"Emily," Miss James said.

My foot itched inside my sneaker. I stepped on it with my other foot to keep it quiet. "Yes?"

Miss James just stood looking at me like she couldn't remember what she wanted to say. After a long time, she shook her head. "Never mind."

I walked backwards to my cubby so I could mind-probe her with my eyes but I didn't find anything.

Miss James clapped her hands. "Everyone bundle up warm. The snow is pretty but it is very cold." She walked around the room and checked people's hats and coats and gloves to make sure they weren't trying to open up and let cold germs in.

Finally she said we could go. I turned into an Olympic skater and hurried outside so I could get my gold medal.

Leigh panted. "Emily. Slow down."

I changed from a skier to an ice skater and spun around on one foot. I saw Joey's hand out of the side of my eye but it was too late. Snow flew away from his fingers and hit me in the face. I fell back.

Leigh was giggling. She hid it behind her hand when she saw me looking at her. It got through anyway, it hit me on the chest and hurt worse than the snow. I stared at her. She looked away.

A car honked. "Leigh. Emily," Leigh's mom said. "Taxi's here."

I locked photon torpedoes on Leigh. She moved her eyes over me and out of range. "C'mon." She ran to the car. I kicked snow at Joey before I followed her.

Leigh's mom was leaning on the car door. "Well, hello there," she said. "How was school today?"

Leigh pointed to a loose paint chip. "Look. The car's bleeding."

"Someone must have bumped it by mistake in the shopping center. No biggie. Here, Emily, let me help you."

I let her.

Leigh's mom slammed the doors shut. I leaned against the window and watched snow swirling down from the clouds. What if the car got frozen shut with us inside? I made a circle in the fog on the window just in case.

Leigh's mom started the car and pulled away from the curb. "I got our tree today. It's a really big one. You'll have to help us decorate one day, Emily."

Leigh twisted her hood string around her finger. "Is Daddy coming for Christmas?"

Leigh's mom didn't answer. I pushed my face against the window and watched all the cars going by to see if anyone was gonna crash. No one did.

"Well?" Leigh said.

"I think this is your block, Emily." Leigh's mom put on her turn signal. It went click click click in time with the windshield wipers.

I looked at Leigh. She stared into space and chewed her shirt collar.

Leigh's mom undid my seatbelt. "That doesn't belong in your mouth, Leigh." She held out her arm. "Careful. There's ice in front of the steps." She squeezed my arm so hard it hurt.

Leigh curled up by the window like a baby.

"See you tomorrow," I said.

Leigh shrugged.

Leigh's mom pulled me towards my house. My feet wanted to slip out from under me but she wouldn't let them. "You guys must have had a really long day," she said. I pretended not to hear. She squeezed my arm tighter than tight until Mama opened the door.

"Did you remember to thank Mrs. Olsen?" Mama said. I nodded even though I hadn't.

I didn't wipe my boots before I came in, but Mama didn't notice. She yawned, for the first time ever I saw that her back teeth were gold instead of white. Maybe someone else was disguised as Mama. I took a step back just in case.

"How was school?" Mama asked through her yawn.

I squinted to see if her face looked like a mask. "Fine."

Mama rubbed her eyes. "Alex is in the kitchen. Go watch him, will you?"

I backwards walked into the kitchen. The steps squeaked, then Mama stomped over my head. Alex banged a spoon on his tray. I ignored him.

Finally it was quiet upstairs. I tiptoed to the window and opened the curtains. "There. It's nice to have light in here." I turned towards Alex. I was Miss James now. "Who can tell us what kind of weather we are having?"

Alex rolled his eyes into the top of his head.

"Eyes forward," I said. Alex ignored me. I sighed. "That's right. It's snowing."

I pressed my nose against the window. Snow fell and fell and fell. I stared harder and wondered what Leigh was doing right now.

Alex made baby noises. I tried to watch him in the window but it wasn't dark enough out, I couldn't see his reflection. I turned around again.

Alex said something in baby language and looked away. I said again, "Eyes forward, Alex." But he wouldn't look at me.

I tiptoed to the refrigerator and got the milk out. I wasn't Miss James anymore, now I was a magic teacher who knew how to mix potions. I drank out of the container. Then I reached behind the dishes in the cabinet to get the Big Bird bottle Mama hid when she wanted me to stop being a baby.

The milk was heavy, maybe the magic was inside it. I hummed a snow spell under my breath and filled Big Bird up.

"Don't worry," I told Big Bird. "Alex won't hurt you." I put him down on Alex's tray.

Alex's eyes turned into pool balls. He shrieked and rocked back and forth so hard that the high chair moved, I was afraid it would fall over.

I grabbed Big Bird and hugged him tight. Alex banged his head against the tray and screamed.

I backed out of the kitchen. Then I turned and ran up the steps.

Mama's room was closed. I wasn't allowed to come in. I squeezed my eyes shut and turned the doorknob anyway.

Mama was lying in the middle of the bed. The blanket rose and fell and rose and fell around her. I tapped her with Big Bird. "Mama?"

"Huh?" Mama said in a sleepy voice.

"Alex's being bad."

Mama said something in sleep language.

I shook her. "Mama, Alex—"

Mama rolled over.

I backed away. "I'm going to go get Uncle Max."

"OK," Mama's voice was still sleepy. She began snoring.

I ran into my room. My stuffed animals stared at me as I got my backpack ready. I didn't care.

I took Patrick the Elephant off the bed. He didn't want to go, he roared loud, but I put him in the front of my backpack anyway. I put Big Bird in the side pocket and zipped both parts just enough so they'd be safe.

Patrick roared while I put on the backpack and went downstairs and got my outside things on. He didn't stop roaring 'til we were outside.

I was an explorer now, I had to find out everything that came between here and Uncle Max's house. I dragged my feet to the end of the street to make tracks so I wouldn't get lost.

There was a big snow bank at the corner. I climbed on it but I couldn't get down again, I had to sit down and slide into the street like I was riding a sled. When I got across, I walked for a long time without getting close to Uncle Max's block.

Patrick shivered. I looked behind me, but I couldn't see my house anymore. All I could see was snow, snow, snow.

I stopped being an explorer and turned into one of the soldiers at Valley Forge. I marched big marching steps so the British couldn't get me. Halfway down the block, I finally saw Uncle Max's building. My feet were tired but I made them run.

When I got there, I stood on my tiptoes to read the little names on the doorbell box. It was all last names, I didn't know Uncle Max's other name, but Patrick said he thought Uncle Max lived in apartment 4B. I pushed that doorbell and held it in for a long time.

No one answered.

I tapped my fingers on the top of the doorbell box to keep them warm. A lady pushing a stroller came out of the building. She smiled and held the door open for me. I slid past her so she wouldn't know I don't live here.

Now that we knew where we were, Patrick calmed down and blew happy flute notes through his trunk. I walked up the steps and down the hall and up more steps. I walked 'til I got to the last little bit of hallway, then I ran. I could hear a basketball game on the TV. Uncle Max was probably sitting in his most specialest chair and drinking a soda, I wanted to jump in his lap like a cat.

The door was open. I tiptoed up to it and looked inside.

No one was there.

What if robbers came and took Uncle Max away? I stood in the doorway just in case.

Footsteps came down the hall. Patrick hid his head in the backpack. I kneeled behind the TV chair and took out Big Bird and sucked in milk.

Uncle Max came in. He threw his laundry sack on the floor and plopped down in the chair. He dug around in the chair pocket for something. Big Bird wanted to see, I craned my neck like a seagull.

Uncle Max was holding a little pipe. He smacked it on the palm of his hand. Then he took a green thing out of his pocket, it looked like the baby leaves the trees get in spring. Uncle Max squashed the baby leaf into the pipe and lit it. It smelled sweet like the pine trees in the woods near Grandma's house. He coughed hard anyway.

I stood up. "You shouldn't smoke. It's bad for you."

Uncle Max hid the pipe in his hand. His eyes slid over me. "Fancy meeting you here. How'd you end up in this part of town?"

I rubbed my right foot on the side of my left foot. "Well," I said, and thought about Alex. My heart beat fast. I didn't want Uncle Max to hate me.

Uncle Max turned the TV down. "Come on. Out with it."

I turned away but Uncle Max's eyes were heat magnets, they found me and burned lasers in my back.

"You're having a hard time," Uncle Max said. His words slid all over each other on the way out of his mouth.

"No, I'm not. But Patrick is, kind of."

Uncle Max giggled. "It must be pretty important for Patrick to make you take him all the way over here. I mean, it's snowing." He patted his lap. "Whatever it is, climb on up."

Patrick roared loud but I ignored him and got on Uncle Max's lap. Uncle Max hugged me. I leaned against him to see if he still felt like Uncle Max. He did.

His heart beat strong in my ears. I sat and listened while I thought about everything. Then I said, "Leigh signed my note."

Uncle Max's chest shook with giggling. I pulled my head away.

"What note?" Uncle Max said.

"This note. Patrick thinks it's trouble."

"Well, then it probably is. Here, I want to see it."

I gave my note to Uncle Max. He stared at it and moved his mouth like he didn't remember how to read.

I turned Big Bird towards me. "Can you sign it?"

"Me sign your note? But I'm not your parent."

"But you have to. Mama keeps forgetting and anyway, Patrick's afraid of her."

"Afraid of her? Nah, that's silly." On the TV, Shaquille O'Neal jumped up and shoved the basketball through the hoop. "Hey, think the Heat's gonna win?" Uncle Max said.

Big Bird turned back into a baby bottle. I slid off Uncle Max's lap and put the bottle in my mouth.

Uncle Max yawned. "I sure wish I could help. I don't think it would count anyway, all things considered."

I kicked my feet in the air. "Would too." Uncle Max ignored me. I kicked his chair. "You're mean. You could help me and you don't. It's not fair. It's not fair. It's not fair."

"You think that's gonna work?" I squirmed but Uncle Max kept his laser beams focused on me, I couldn't escape.

The phone rang.

"I'll get that," Uncle Max said. "You calm down."

I watched Uncle Max go in the kitchen. My throat felt tighter than tight, my heart beat fast. I poked Patrick and crawled around the chair. There was a plastic bag in the pocket, it was full of baby leaves.

I told Patrick to stand lookout while I took a leaf out and sniffed it. On the phone Uncle Max said my name. I stretched my hearing 'til my ears ached, but I couldn't get the rest of what he was saying.

Uncle Max came out of the kitchen. He stood up straight as a fireman's pole. "You left Alex alone?"

The leaf fell out of my hand. Uncle Max looked at me.There was no more laughing in his eyes. They were big and black like Alex's.

I kicked at the rug like a cat in the litter box. "I was gonna tell you."

"Look at me, Emily." Uncle Max's voice pulled my head to him like a puppet on a rope. "Your mom's on her way over. She's pretty mad at us. So we gotta stand strong, OK?"

My shoe had a long lace. I watched it sweep the floor. "OK."

Uncle Max stood looking at me, it was like he wanted to say something else but forgot how.

"Uncle Max? Why is Mama mad at us?"

"Cause . . . well . . ." Someone made loud footsteps outside, they made Uncle Max's eyes get big and round. "I can't tell you just now."

The footsteps went away. Uncle Max let his breath out slowly. "Quick. Let me see that note again."

I took stiff robot steps towards Uncle Max. He read the note fast, his reading brain was working again. When he was done he shook his head. "So much like me." Before I could ask him what he meant he added, "Your mom's not gonna be too happy about this, kiddo."

"I told you. Can't you just sign it?"

"I wish I could. You're just gonna have to take your lumps from your mom. She's not gonna understand, but you'll live." He read the note again. "Why couldn't you just sing the stupid songs?"

I stared at the floor. "God didn't want me to." Uncle Max didn't say anything. "Really, He didn't. Those songs were all about—"

Just then someone pressed the outside doorbell hard and held it in. It buzzed so loud I couldn't think, even when I put my hands over my ears.

Uncle Max pressed the button to open the door. "About Jesus, right?"

An elephant stomped up the steps and made the house shake. I wanted to hide behind Uncle Max, but I just nodded.

"Here." Uncle Max gave me back the note. "Give this to your mom and get it over with." He ruffled my hair.

The elephant came to the door and held the doorbell in. Uncle Max's hand fell out of my hair. He walked fast to the door.

I knelt down by the chair. I was a little mouse checking for cats from my secret hiding place.

Mama stormed in. "Where is she?" She stomped towards the chair. I made myself flat so she couldn't squash me.

"Calm down, will you?" Uncle Max said.

Mama whirled around. "Don't tell me what to do. And get Emily. Now." She wrinkled up her nose. Her eyes caught fire and spit it at Uncle Max but she said something so quiet I couldn't hear.

Uncle Max nodded just a little bit. "I'm sorry. I didn't know. I stopped as soon as she came up."

Mama stared at Uncle Max 'til his head drooped down. I hugged Big Bird to me so he wouldn't see.

Mama's middle went up and down like an accordion. "Where is my daughter?" She threw her purse down so hard it bounced. "Emily. Come on out. It's time to go." Her voice was soft like the witch in Hansel and Gretel.

I crawled forward a little bit and stuck my head out. Mama's face was mad, but she was smiling. I ducked back again and held my breath.

"Come on, Emily," Mama said. "I'm giving you 'til three."

I let my breath out. It pushed me all the way out into the open.

Mama turned towards me as I stood up. I didn't like her fire-eyes on me. I pretended to be looking at some white dust on my jeans.

"Thank God," Mama said. I put the Big Bird bottle in my mouth. Mama's lips got tight. "Give me that bottle so we ca go."

I shielded Big Bird with my elbow. “Patrick wants to say goodbye to Uncle Max.”

Mama’s eyes flashed but her smile got bigger. “Of course he does.” I looked away. “Well? Say it.”

I looked at Uncle Max for help. His eyes were two big, black holes that didn’t even see me, they only saw empty space.

“Uncle Max?”

Uncle Max squeezed my shoulder. “Go with your mom, OK?”

“But—”

“Come on already,” Mama said. I started to follow her out of the room but I was looking at Uncle Max. He was staring into the pipe like it was the Black Cauldron.

Mama was too busy walking to see, she was already halfway down the hall. I stopped in the doorway. “Uncle Max? Patrick wants to know—”

The hallway shook as Mama came back. Uncle Max shoved the pipe into his pocket.

“Now, Emily.” Mama said. “Daddy’s waiting.”

I ran to Uncle Max and hugged him tight. He whispered, “We’ll talk soon. I promise.”

I didn’t want to let him go.

I could feel Mama’s eyes drilling holes in me. I went towards her before she could melt me into a pile of nothing.

Patrick stayed quiet in the backpack.

Outside it was snowing again. I didn’t care.

FOUR

Snow swirled around and around as I followed Mama to the car. It got in my hair and under my coat collar and on my boots. Mama got in the car and sat still like she was frozen. I knocked snow away from the window. She flinched and let me in.

Mama drove away. The windshield wipers scratched loud on the front window.

I held Patrick tight on my lap. "Where's Daddy?"

"Huh?"

I kicked at the seat to wake Mama up. "You said Daddy's waiting. Where is he?"

"I never said any such thing, Emily." Mama turned the heat knob. "Now be quiet so I can drive."

"You did too. Big Bird heard you."

Mama choked the steering wheel. "I said be quiet," she said in a tornado voice. "Now shut up."

My throat got tight. I turned towards the window and rubbed off snow fuzz to make a pattern. It turned into a mess.

I pushed my lips tight together and looked out the window. Three blocks, two blocks, one.

"You passed our block, Mama."

Mama sped up a little. The car jerked forward like it had just woke up. "We're not going home, Emily."

I hugged Patrick tighter. "Where are we going?"

"You are going to Leigh's house."

"But what—"

"I have something to do."

Patrick made his trunk into a question mark. I looked out the window but he was whining so I turned back around. "Why couldn't I stay at Uncle Max's then?"

Mama turned on the radio. “It takes forever to get anywhere in this snow,” she said to an invisible somebody. I didn’t answer.

When we got to Leigh’s block, Mama took her phone out of the thing in between the front seats and pressed it so hard on her ear I was afraid it would get stuck. I held my breath while she called Leigh’s mom to say we were here. I didn’t let it out ’til she put the phone away.

“Listen up, Emily,” Mama said. “Leigh and her mom don’t know a lot about our family and they don’t need to. So don’t say anything to them about Alex or Uncle Max or . . . or anything that happened today. Got it?”

I nodded even though I had no idea what Mama was talking about.

Leigh’s mom came towards the car. I could kind of see her through the fogged-up window. She looked like a fuzz ball.

Mama turned around like she hadn’t just been talking to me. She rolled the window down. The wind roared in just cause it could.

“Hi,” she said. I couldn’t see her, Leigh’s mom was in the way, but I knew she had her smile face on. “Well, here we are.”

Leigh’s mom said something I couldn’t hear. I unbuckled my seatbelt and moved up.

Mama cut her conversation in half. “Go inside, Emily. And leave your elephant here. You don’t need it.”

I hugged Patrick tight and walked away.

“Emily!”

“Oh, let her keep him,” Leigh’s mom said. I ducked behind a tree to listen to the rest of their conversation.

Leigh’s mom leaned in closer. She said something about the hospital. Mama said she was meeting Daddy there.

Leigh's mom sighed and got up. I jumped away from the tree and got ahead of her. "The door's locked."

"Just push it without turning the knob. You know that." Leigh's mom shoved herself against the door, it opened up. I tossed my hair back and stepped carefully inside. I was the Queen of England coming off the plane for a visit.

"Why don't you go up to Leigh's room and put Patrick down for a nap?" Leigh's mom asked.

I hugged Patrick tight. "Where's Leigh?"

"Oh, she's around somewhere." Leigh's mom went to the basement steps. "Leigh." Leigh didn't answer. Her mom moved through the house like a surfer. "Leigh. Emily's here." She spun towards me on invisible ice skates. "You can do your homework on this table. Leigh did hers already. I know it won't take you long." She slid towards the upstairs steps. "I really think Patrick would be more comfortable on the bed, don't you?"

Leigh came to the top of the steps. She had a sour look on. "I was writing to Daddy."

"Oh, honey . . ." Leigh's mom put on her biggest smile. "That can wait a while, don't you think?"

Leigh locked laser beams on me. "What are you doing here?"

"Leigh. That's no way to behave. I apologize, Emily, for Leigh's rudeness."

Leigh took a robot step closer. "Well?"

Leigh's mom put her hand on my shoulder. I made my back stiff but she didn't let go. "Why don't you get started on your homework?" she said.

I kicked out the chair and sat down. Leigh's mom turned around. "Emily's parents had to take her brother to the hospital. So I don't care that you've been in a mood since I picked you up from school today. You will be nice to her until her mom gets back."

I shoved my hand into a side pocket and grabbed Big Bird. *Alex . . . I'm sorry . . .* Leigh's mom was looking at me. I let Big Bird go and pretended to be doing my homework.

"Finish up, Emily," Leigh's mom said. "Then we can decorate the tree. Leigh, honey, please get the ornaments."

Leigh pouted but she went anyway.

I put Patrick on the chair next to me and opened up my homework notebook. Miss James had wrote different colors in marker, we were supposed to find pictures to match the colors.

"Here's some magazines," Leigh's mom said. "You find the pictures, I'll cut them out." I opened up a magazine. "And Emily? Don't let Leigh upset you, OK?"

I shrugged. "Red, red, red." The magazine was full of red somethings. Red was everywhere. It made me think of ambulances.

I squeezed my eyes shut to get away from all that red. Leigh came up the steps. I heard her go thump, thump, crash.

"More gently, please," Leigh's mom said. "We don't want anything to break."

I did my homework. Leigh's mom took the scissors away and cut the pictures for me. I didn't care. I was watching Leigh. She sat on the couch with her arms crossed, staring at the place where the TV would be if there was one.

Patrick asked why Leigh was sad.

"Mrs. Olsen?" I said. "What time is my mom coming back?"

"Soon." Leigh's mom squeezed my shoulder. "Are you done with that? Good. Let's decorate."

I got up slowly. Leigh watched me through the invisible TV. Her mom opened up the ornament box. "Look, girls. Santa's reindeer." She pushed the box towards me.

My heart beat faster than fast. I put my hand under my shirt to calm it down. "But we don't celebrate Christmas at my house."

"So what? You're in my house right now, and in my house you do."

Leigh's head jerked up. "Did you tell my mom about your note?"

I shook my head.

"Ah, who cares?" Leigh's mom said. "Come on, let's decorate."

Leigh got on her knees to look in the ornament box. "Emily got a note home," she said. "When Miss James said sing *Silent Night* she didn't, she just pretended."

I put my teeth together. "Be quiet."

"If Daddy were here he would spank her, right, Mommy?"

Leigh's mom wrapped a long piece of silver foil around a tall branch. "Oh, who knows what that father of yours would do. Come on, girls. Am I doing this all by myself?"

Leigh picked up a statue of a man on a fat white cross. "Look, Emily. It's Jesus." She shoved the ornament at me. I stared over it at the wall so God wouldn't know I saw it.

"Leigh." Leigh's mom wrapped the foil behind the branch and over the next one.

"Here, Mommy. Put this at the very top."

"It's too heavy. The tree will topple over." Leigh's mom wrapped the last little bit of foil around the top of the tree. "Emily, help us out. Ornaments don't bite, you know."

I took a baby step towards the tree. Patrick was so scared he slid off his chair.

Leigh's mom started singing *Deck the Halls* as she took an ornament out of the box. I made myself flat so the song couldn't get me. Leigh started singing too. Her voice was very quiet. In the middle of the song she began to cry.

Leigh's mom squeezed an ornament like it was an orange. "Honey, don't . . . ," she said. Leigh sniffed and wiped her nose on her shirt. Her mom didn't tell her not to.

The phone rang.

Leigh's mom smiled so wide her smile got stuck. "Oh, Emily, maybe that's your mom." She ran into the kitchen.

Leigh pushed her feet all the way into the bottom of the couch. I pushed myself up so I was standing big and tall. "Wanna hold Patrick 'til you feel better?"

Leigh shoved Patrick away. "Leave me alone." She kicked the couch. I stared at the floor. All of a sudden Leigh said, "Emily? Come sit with me?"

I took a couple of steps towards the couch. Leigh kicked it harder than hard. "Psst," she said, beckoning me. I bent down and she whispered in my ear, "I'm inviting Daddy for Christmas. Don't tell my mom."

In the kitchen, Leigh's mom laughed.

Leigh kicked the couch twice as hard. "That new family's not gonna be here 'til July. And guess what? They have a stupid boy." She glared at the floor.

Before I could say anything, Leigh's mom turned into a ballerina and danced into the room. "Good news, Emily. Your daddy's on his way. Leigh, if you're going to kick the couch, please take off your shoes."

Leigh kicked her shoes off so hard they flew up and hit the wall. Her mom turned around and said in a smiley voice, "Here, Emily, let's get your things so we won't keep your daddy waiting."

Leigh slid off the couch.

"Say goodbye to Emily," her mom said.

Leigh stomped across the room and up the steps.

"I'm sorry Leigh's being so rude," Leigh's mom said. "She's—"

A car outside went honk honk honk like a flock of geese.

"There's your daddy." Leigh's mom opened the door.

Patrick was afraid I'd forget him. I picked him up so he knew I never ever would.

Daddy drove like a slowpoke turtle. When we got home, he cleared his throat and looked at me. His eyes were little and sad, they had sleep lines on them.

I held Patrick tight against me. "Daddy?"

Daddy yawned. "Well, we're home." He got out.

I leaned over and opened the door a little bit.

"Wait, wait." Daddy put his hand on the door handle, but instead of opening it he squeezed it and looked at something far away in the sky. I tilted my head back 'til it wouldn't go any further. I couldn't see anything.

Daddy sighed and pulled the door open all the way. "Better go in. It's cold."

I tiptoed out of the car and up the path. I was a North Pole explorer, I had to be careful of enemy spies from a different country.

"Let's go, Emily." Daddy's voice was cold as the wind.

We went inside. I didn't see Mama anywhere, but I wiped my boots on the mat anyway, just in case. Daddy didn't wipe his. I pretended not to see.

I took off my coat and dropped it on the floor. Daddy picked it up and put it on its hook.

"Don't disappear," Daddy said. "We have to have a talk."

I took a half step back. "Come with me into the dining room," Daddy said.

In the dining room, Daddy tossed a box of candles on the table. "Pick out colors. Hurry up."

I took out a green candle, a white candle, and a yellow candle. Three candles for winter, spring, and summer. "Sorry, orange candle," I said. "You don't get to go yet." I tried to put the candles in the menorah but they jumped out. Daddy grabbed my wrist and pushed down so hard it hurt. He scared the candles so they stayed where they belonged.

Daddy lit the candles. He stood and stared into the flame. "So," he said. "I heard you went for a walk today."

I took a step back. "Where's Mama?"

"She's on her way back. With Alex." Daddy came towards me. "Who said you could leave?" He came closer, I backed away 'til I hitted the wall. "Aren't you only six years old?"

I tried to make myself smaller but I couldn't, Daddy was standing too close. I squinted to make him less big. "The prayer, Daddy."

Daddy choked the table with his fist. "Yeah. The prayer." He went over to the other side of the table. His back was stiff and straight and angry. I looked away.

Daddy sang in a soft robot voice, it was worse than me in music class. I tiptoed away and got my note. I wanted to show it to Daddy but instead I held it tight and stared at the flame.

Mama opened the front door. I jumped even though I knew it was her.

"Oh good, you guys are home." Mama's voice was flat as a robot soldier. "I'll start dinner in a minute. Let me just put Alex down."

"No, you've had a hard day," Daddy told her. "Let me help."

Mama's eyes widened. She rubbed Alex's back, he made himself limp like an old rag doll.

"Here," Daddy said. "I'll put him in the high chair."

Alex screamed as soon as Daddy touched him. Daddy pushed him in the high chair like he was a jack-in-the-box that got out.

"Dan?" Mama said. "Did you talk to Emily?"

Daddy pulled the high chair tray out. "There. That's not so bad, is it?" He turned towards Mama. "A little, yeah."

"Did you explain—"

Daddy nodded at me over Mama's shoulder. She swallowed up the rest of her sentence and put her head close to Daddy's so they could talk.

I dropped to my knees and put Patrick on my back. I crawled closer but I couldn't hear. Patrick fell off me.

Daddy's hand fell off Mama's shoulder like a leaf in the fall. "Get up, Emily. Mama needs help setting the table."

I put Patrick in his chair. Daddy said, "Uh uh. That toy goes away."

"But Patrick's starving, Daddy. He's waiting for his dinner."

Daddy took great big breaths like a fish. "It goes away. Or else it goes in the garbage."

I grabbed Patrick and held him tight against me so no one could hurt him. "Don't worry. Daddy didn't mean it." I backed into the kitchen, watching Daddy, just in case.

Mama and Daddy went back to whispering. Me and Patrick crouched by the sink and held each other while we tried to listen. After a long time, Mama's chair scraped the floor and Mama came in the kitchen.

I got up.

"Have you been sitting there all this time?" Mama said. She rubbed the headache spot on the top of her nose. "Get started, please. Dinner's late enough as it is. And put that elephant down. It's in your way."

I hugged Patrick as tight as I could without cutting off his breath. "I can't. Daddy wants to throw him away."

"No, he doesn't. That's ridiculous." Mama locked photon torpedoes on me but I didn't move. "Here. I'll put it on your bed for you so you'll have it when you're ready to go to sleep."

I backed away.

"Emily, please," Mama said. "It's late. Give me the stupid elephant so you can set the table."

Mama was smiling. I checked her eyes for secret fire, but they were just gray and tired. She breathed deeper than deep. "Please don't make me ask Daddy to come in here," she said.

I hugged Patrick one last time. "Make sure to tuck him in tight the way he likes," I said, but Mama was already walking away.

I pulled the silverware drawer open and took out 3 forks and 3 spoons. I didn't want to touch the knives.

When I came into the dining room, Daddy was sitting and staring into the candles. "Daddy?" I said. "Are you talking to God?"

"What?" Daddy rubbed his eyes like he was waking up from a dream. "Of course not. Jews don't pray that way."

"How do they pray?"

Mama was coming in the room so Daddy didn't answer. Instead he pushed his chair back and said, "Come on, let's all pitch in to get dinner made. Emily, follow me."

Mama stared hard at me. "Someone needs to watch Alex."

"Sit down and relax, then," Daddy said. "Emily and I—"

Mama banged the table so hard the menorah wobbled. "Relax? Me?" She laughed. "Day in, day out, I'm worrying. I'm taking him to doctors. I'm watching him. And you're telling me to relax?"

Daddy's eyes caught fire from the candles. "Fine. You make dinner, then." Mama's eyes got hard as ice. "What?"

"Nothing. Emily's not a baby anymore, that's all. Why can't—"

"Because of this afternoon. She can't be trusted. And apparently, neither can you."

Mama took a big breath like Daddy's words punched her in the stomach. She stared down at the table.

Daddy turned his fire-eyes on me before I could duck. "You. Get in the kitchen."

I ran. I closed the kitchen door behind me and locked it with an invisible lock. Mama said something but Daddy shouted loud to erase her voice. Alex shrieked once, then he was quiet.

I crawled under the kitchen table, it was a cool cave with a lake in the middle. It made me feel safe.

After a long time it got quiet outside. I poked my head out, I didn't see any monsters. The quiet stayed. I got up and went into the dining room.

Alex was under the table, he had made himself flat like a scared cat. No one was paying any attention to him. Instead, Daddy was rubbing Mama's shoulders. "I know you're overwhelmed," he said. "That's why I thought we'd make you dinner tonight."

I squatted down and tried to pat Alex. He shrieked and slid away. "Be a nice cat," I said.

"Here, Emily." Daddy got up. "I'll get your brother."

I crawled out from under the table. Daddy dived in like an undersea explorer looking for treasure. Alex screamed and kicked and even tried to bite. Daddy took him away from the table anyway.

The phone rang.

Daddy yawned. “That could be a patient. Make sure Alex doesn’t retreat back under the table.”

Mama’s lips got tight but she just looked at the table and said, “OK.”

I tried to put Alex in a force field with my eyes but he turned away. My stomach ached with hunger. I rubbed it to keep from growling.

“Maybe we can order a pizza,” Mama said. I watched her reflection in the window. Her face looked like it was on too tight. She rubbed the sides of her head like the tightness was hurting her and smiled a pretend smile. “With all this snow, it’ll be bedtime before they get it here.”

I didn’t say anything back. I was too busy listening to Daddy on the phone.

“This is Emily’s father.” Daddy tapped the phone cord on the wall. “No, I wasn’t aware of the situation.”

Daddy opened the door and bent his head around it like a snake. Mama was staring at the window without seeing anything. She didn’t move.

“No,” Daddy said. “My wife is not available. However, you can talk to me.” He laughed. “I’m an enlightened man. I help with the kids.”

I climbed off my seat and tiptoed into the kitchen.

Daddy twisted the phone cord round his finger. “Emily did what? No, no, my wife would have mentioned . . . I’m sure she didn’t see any note.”

I tugged on Daddy’s shirt bottom. He pushed me away. “I wanna talk to Miss James.”

Daddy put his finger on his lips. “Well, you know, I hope it doesn’t come to that. I don’t want—”

I pulled on Daddy’s shirt harder. “Let me talk.”

Daddy turned towards me. He looked like a werewolf, his eyes were black and mean and wild and he breathed through his teeth.

I forgot I was Jewish and started crossing myself in case Daddy wanted to bite me.

Daddy breathed deep. He turned back into himself and said in a quiet voice, "Go wait in the dining room."

I backed away. The kitchen door swung closed by itself and almost hit me.

Mama was singing to Alex but she stopped. "Don't slam the door, Emily."

I leaned against the wall and tried to listen to Daddy. "I'm starving."

"I know." Mama opened the kitchen door a crack. "Dan."

"I'm on the phone." Daddy's voice was a hurricane, it made Mama wobble and almost fall down. She jumped back.

The door closed. Mama grabbed it so it didn't slam. "You'll have to wait."

After a minute, Daddy came out of the kitchen. "Sorry about that. Emily—"

Mama cleared her throat. "Could you make the kids eggs since it's so late?"

Daddy breathed in so hard his body shook. "Fine. Emily can help me." Mama started to say something, but Daddy shot fire at her with his eyes and she went back to staring at the tablecloth.

"Mama?" I said.

Mama didn't look up. "Go help your father," she said. Her voice was so low it made my ears hurt.

I squeezed my tummy to make myself strong before going in the kitchen.

Daddy was taking a pan out from next to the stove. He glanced at me. "Take the eggs out of the refrigerator."

I got the eggs and tiptoed with them towards Daddy, I was a ballerina doing a complicated dance on stage. "Here."

Daddy cracked an egg on the pan. "So," he said. "Tell me about this note."

I squirmed. "Well . . ."

"I don't know what 'well' means." Daddy stirred the eggs with a spatula. "Never mind. Give me your note. And get me the jelly, too."

I took the jelly out and hugged it as hard as I could without breaking it. Daddy grabbed it out of my hands. He dug into it with a spoon like he was unburying a pile of gold.

Daddy flipped the eggs onto a plate. I reached for it, but he cleared his throat loud.

"I want that note, Emily," Daddy said.

I put my hand in my pocket, I was a fishing rod and the note was a fish. Daddy grabbed it out of my hand so hard it started to rip.

I held my breath while Daddy read the note. He lifted his head very, very slowly. I let my breath out.

"So." Daddy hit the note against his palm. "You—"

The kitchen door swung open so fast it hit the wall behind him. Mama came in. "Alex's hungry, Dan. He's squirming and rocking."

Daddy pushed the plate towards me. "Bring this to your brother."

Heat soaked through the bottom of the plate and tried to burn me.

"Hurry up," Daddy said.

I backed out of the room. I was a waitress in a famous restaurant and I couldn't drop the plate.

Daddy leaned over and closed the door as soon as I was gone.

I put the plate down on the table. "Here you go, sir." Alex didn't answer. I cut the eggs in half with my spoon, jelly bled out onto the plate.

Alex pressed his head into the table. He said something but I couldn't tell if it was baby language or regular, his words melted into the table like he never said them.

I ate the jelly and cut the eggs into squares.

One of the squares was all white somehow. Alex reached over and grabbed it. He turned it over and over.

Outside, the sky turned the snow into a big roll of thunder. Then it was quiet.

Inside, the candles burned almost all the way to the bottom and bled onto the menorah.

I ate the eggs. They burned my throat on the way down.

FIVE

When I woke up Monday, I thought it was still night cause it was dark in my room. I could hear Mama putting dishes away. She sounded mad, she kept slamming them.

I tiptoed to the top step and sat down.

"Rain again," Mama said, and Daddy answered, "Are you sure you want to go all the way out to Levittown in this weather?"

"I have to." Mama slammed a drawer. "Alex has an appointment."

Daddy said something I couldn't hear.

"Emily," Mama called. "Are you dressed?"

I crawled back to my room and picked out a shirt and a pair of striped jeans.

Mama threw my door open without knocking. I pulled my pants up fast as I could.

"Daddy's going to take you to school on his way to work," Mama said. She stood staring at me.

I looked away. "What?"

"Your clothes don't match."

Alex made a funny almost-crying sound from the next room. Mama looked over her shoulder. "Dan?" Daddy didn't answer. Mama sighed. "Change your pants," she said, and went down the hall.

I looked in the mirror. My clothes didn't look funny to me.

I went downstairs.

Daddy was reading the newspaper. "Here." He slid my note across the table. "Don't lose that."

I walked behind Daddy to see what he was reading. He leaned forward to block the words. "Go get yourself breakfast, please."

I stuck my lip all the way out but I didn't make a hole in Daddy's energy shield. "Mama always makes it for me."

"I put the cereal on the bottom shelf so you can reach it."

I dragged my feet to the cupboard, I was one of the slave Jews escaping in the desert. As I opened it, I realized God didn't like me being a slave. I turned into Miss James teaching us how to make cereal for snack time.

Mama came in as I was showing an invisible class how to pour milk. "Almost ready?" she said to Daddy.

Daddy didn't look up. "Put Alex down. I'll feed him."

Mama dropped Alex in Daddy's lap and took two giant steps towards me. "That milk's too heavy for you, Emily. You'll spill it."

"But Daddy said—"

"Let Mama pour it." Daddy turned the page. Alex whimpered and tried to get away but Daddy held him tighter.

I didn't like the way Daddy was squeezing Alex's wrist. I watched Mama pour the milk instead. It dripped down like clouds turned into liquid.

"Here you go," Mama said in her smile voice. She pushed the bowl towards me.

The milk spilled.

"Damn it." Mama pushed a spoon into my hand. "Eat this right here so it doesn't spill."

I didn't answer. I was watching Alex. He was twisting and fighting Daddy's arms, he was mad for no reason. I squinted at him to try to read his mind but he was moving too much, my eyes kept falling off him.

"Earth to Emily," Mama said. She took two baby steps towards Daddy. "Put him in the high chair, Dan."

"No, Rebekah. He's got to learn to sit properly."

Mama bit her lip. She drilled holes in Daddy with her eyes, but he didn't budge.

I stirred my cereal and made the milk splash out. No one paid any attentions to me. Alex crawled out of Daddy's lap. He went under the table and made himself flat.

The doorbell rang.

Mama went to get it. "Oh, come in, Leigh. Emily's daddy will be ready in just a minute."

I dropped to my knees and crawled out of the kitchen.

"Oh, why can't we walk?" Leigh said.

Mama pinched her lips together. "It's too cold out."

Leigh took baby steps into the living room. I jumped up. "Boo!"

Leigh stared at the floor. "Hi, Emily." Her shoe had a long lace, she made it go round and round. "I'm sorry about yesterday."

"What happened yesterday?" Mama asked.

Leigh wiped circles on the floor with her sneakers.

I followed her foot with my head. "Isn't Daddy ready yet?"

Leigh's eyes got wide. "Oh, I want to walk. Don't you, Emily?"

I twisted my head around and looked out the window. Rain slid down the glass and made it look like it was crying. "I guess."

"Walk in the rain. Walk in the rain." Leigh looked at me. I chanted with her, but in a tiny voice no one could hear.

"Get your backpack, Emily," Mama said.

Me and Leigh kept chanting while I got my backpack and came back and let Mama help me with my outside things. Then a chair scraped in the kitchen and footsteps echoed through the hall.

Daddy came in the room. I stopped chanting.

"Ready, girls?" Daddy opened the door and went out.

I wanted to say goodbye to Mama, but she was already half-way in the kitchen with Alex.

As soon as we got in Daddy's car, Leigh took a fat book out of her backpack and opened it. I tried to look over her shoulder at it but she hugged it to herself.

I looked out the window instead. Everything looked blurry and bent out of shape.

The car crawled along slower than slow. After forever, we got to school. Leigh and her book ran inside without saying Thank You. I said it extra loud for both of us. I wanted to kiss Daddy, too, but as soon as I got out of the car he sped away like he was in a race.

"Everybody inside," the playground teacher said.

Wind and rain followed me as I hurried to Miss James' room, I shivered under my outside things while water dripped off them onto the floor.

"Well!" Miss James said as everyone shuffled into the first grade room. "This is some weather we're having, isn't it?" She squeezed her hands to warm them up. "Who needs help taking off their outside things?"

I pulled my gloves off hard and threw them on the floor. Miss James was looking so I picked them up again.

After everyone's outside things were tucked away safe in the cubbies, we did the Pledge of Allegiance and sang *My Country 'Tis of Thee*. This time I sang all the words.

Miss James cleared her throat. "Boys and girls, please don't sit down yet."

I kicked my chair out and started to sit down anyway. Miss James' eyes were stuck to me. I stood up again.

"There are only three weeks left until the Christmas concert," Miss James said. Her voice was loud and slow like the rain ruined her batteries. "We all need to practice hard so we can have a nice show."

Miss James' eyes sent out magnets and pulled everyone's head towards me. I squeezed my pencil hard in case I needed to break her magic.

"And so," Miss James said, "we are going to have music practice every morning from—"

The little box on the wall by Miss James' desk beeped, someone in Mr. O'Leary's office had pressed the button hard.

Miss James pulled her shirt down even though it was on right. "Yes?" She twisted her head over her shoulder to look at me.

I looked at my desk.

"I haven't had a chance to ask. Oh. I see. Well, we're on our way to the auditorium now."

Miss James let go of the buzzer. Her back was stiff and angry like Mama's, but when she turned around she was herself again, she even had a smile face on. "OK, children," she said. "Let's form an orderly line so we can go to the music room."

Everyone got up at once. Leigh got up so fast her chair fell over. Joey laughed and knocked his over to imitate her. Then all of a sudden, the whole class was doing the same thing.

Except me.

Miss James turned into a vacuum cleaner and whirled around the room, picking up chairs and blowing everyone towards the door. When she got to my desk, she unplugged herself. "I don't suppose you brought your note," she said.

I looked around for enemy spies as I took the note out of my pocket.

Miss James smiled at me. She tapped the note against her palm. "Uhm."

I tilted my head up and waited.

Miss James breathed in but the breath went out of her like she was a leaky balloon. "Thanks for getting this signed," she said.

I squinted at Miss James as she walked away to see if I could find a messed up wire in her brain. I couldn't.

"Come, children," Miss James said. "Let's not waste our time."

Everyone pushed and shoved to be first. I dragged my feet so I could hide in the back of the line. We turned into soldiers and marched to the music room.

Someone had taken all the chairs away from the front of the room and put in three long steps instead. Mr. O'Leary was sitting on the bottom step. He got up when he saw us coming.

Miss James smiled at Mr. O'Leary. He didn't smile back. "Wet day, isn't it?" she said.

Mr. O'Leary scanned Miss James with his eyes. "Have the children line up in size order, please."

"Oh, by the way." Miss James handed Mr. O'Leary the note.

Mr. O'Leary ran his finger across Daddy's signature like he was trying to erase it. Miss James stood still as a wax statue 'til he nodded.

While Miss James was waiting, Joey got on his tiptoes to make himself taller than Leigh. Leigh balanced herself on the very tips of her feet to make them equal. I tried to make myself taller, too, but Joey shoved me.

Miss James turned around before I could shove Joey back. "I am very disappointed, boys and girls." Behind her, Mr.

O'Leary was frowning. "This is not a good use of our music time."

I bounced happy energy off the steps so Miss James would stop being mad.

"Now," Miss James said. "Let's try again to use our time properly. When I call your name, please come up to the risers."

Leigh got called to the second step. I listened hard for my name, but Miss James forgot to call me next. I started to follow Leigh anyway. Miss James didn't let me.

When she was done, Miss James stepped back and looked at us. "OK, that looks good." She sat down at the piano. "You are in for a treat, Mr. O'Leary. The children have been working very hard on their concert songs."

I put my hands on my stomach and pressed it in. The piano echoed in my ears 'til I was afraid I couldn't breathe. I hummed instead of singing so God wouldn't be mad.

Behind me, Joey started jumping up and down to make the risers shake.

Miss James stopped the song in the middle. She breathed hard while she closed the piano lid. "OK, children," she said, pushing the bench back. "Are you done fooling around?"

I looked at the floor.

"We're going to begin again," Miss James said. "Everyone stand still and sing." She spun around on her heel like a Chanukah dreidel.

My heart beat fast. I closed my eyes tight and said the candle prayer in my head. Miss James scraped the piano bench loud against the floor and cut my prayer in half. I opened my eyes and raised my hand.

Miss James opened the piano. "I am not in a discussing mood, Emily." She began counting.

I opened my mouth wide and pressed my tummy in. My tongue felt dryer than dry, a weird whistling sound came out of me like when the wind gets stuck in between the trees.

Miss James looked up but she went on playing. I sang the first three words, but God didn't want me to sing anymore so instead I watched Leigh and opened and closed my mouth when she did so it would look like I was singing.

The bell rang as Miss James played the last note. Everything was quiet, but the bell kept on ringing inside me. Mr. O'Leary frowned at me. Then he got up and clapped.

"Let's go, children," Miss James said. "Emily, come up front with me, please."

"If I may, Miss James," Mr. O'Leary said, "I'd like to borrow Emily for a moment."

Miss James twisted a loose thread around her finger. "It's Emily's turn to be line leader, Mr. O'Leary. Perhaps—"

"I'm afraid that'll have to wait. Follow me, Emily."

Miss James looked like she wanted to say something, but she turned around. "Come, children."

I waited 'til everyone went away before I jumped off the riser.

Mr. O'Leary was quiet the whole way to his office. He stood straight and tall and walked very fast. My legs ached from keeping up with him. A pretend nurse told me to slow down so I wouldn't have to use crutches, but I couldn't or I'd get lost.

When we got there, Miss Green gave Mr. O'Leary some papers, I read them upside down and saw they were full of numbers.

"I can't right now," Mr. O'Leary said. "I have a situation here." He unlocked his office door. "Come, Emily."

I kicked a chair out. It was made of cold metal that made goosebumps grow on my back. Mr. O'Leary reached for a pen without taking his eyes off me. He kept staring while he made some notes in a big book.

I squirmed. "It's not nice to stare."

"Oh?" Mr. O'Leary slammed the book closed. "Do you think your behavior this morning was nice?"

I thought about it. I couldn't remember doing anything unnice, but I knew Mr. O'Leary wanted me to say No so I tried to think harder.

Mr. O'Leary leaned back in his chair. "We both know it wasn't," he said. "Miss James might have overlooked what you were doing, but believe me, I saw everything."

I screwed up my eyes to look in Mr. O'Leary's brain, I couldn't find what he was talking about.

"Don't make faces, Emily. This is not a joke." Mr. O'Leary tapped his fingers on the desk. "Were your parents laughing when they read that note?"

I didn't answer, instead I stared over Mr. O'Leary's shoulder at the window. The wind and rain were shaking a big tree and making it cry.

"I didn't think so. Nor will they be glad to hear about this latest indiscretion." Mr. O'Leary picked up the phone. "Is your mom home?"

I sat up straighter than straight to make myself more grown-up. "She's at an appointment in Levittown. And Daddy's at work." If no one was home Mr. O'Leary would have to call Uncle Max, he was the third number on my emergency card.

"I see." Mr. O'Leary kept his eyes on me as he leaned his chair back. He wanted me to look away but I wouldn't.

"You shouldn't lean back like that," I said. "You might fall over."

Mr. O'Leary rocked back and forth in the chair. He kept staring at me like he was waiting for something. A big gust of wind blew against the window, so hard I thought the glass might break. I squeezed the edge of the desk and said a prayer in my head.

Mr. O'Leary put his chair back on the ground. "I'm too busy for this," he said. "Are you sorry or not?"

"For what?" I stared at my feet and listened to the wind and rain talking to each other.

"Sit up straight," Mr. O'Leary said. I sat up. He tried to trap me with his eyes again, but I looked through him and out the window.

Mr. O'Leary's phone buzzed. "All right," he said. "It's obvious I'm just wasting my time here. Back to class with you." He stood up. His shadow was even taller than he was. It weighed down on me and tried to stop me from standing.

I got up anyway.

Mr. O'Leary scowled and shoved his hands into his pockets. "I'll be back soon," he said to Miss Green. My body felt heavy as I followed him down the hall. I watched my shoelace sweep the floor all the way back to Miss James' room.

When we got there, Mr. O'Leary leaned over me and pulled the door open.

" . . . so when we multiply, it is a shortcut to adding," Miss James was saying. She stopped and turned towards Mr. O'Leary.

"Miss James," Mr. O'Leary said.

Miss James put her chalk down. She wiped her hands on her dress, then she remembered not to and used a paper towel instead. "Yes, Mr. O'Leary?"

"I have some bad news, I'm afraid." Mr. O'Leary looked down at the ground. "Emily does not want to participate in the Christmas concert this year."

Someone said, "Ooh, Emily . . . ," and it echoed through the room like the fire alarm when we have a drill.

Miss James kept wiping her hands. "I'm sorry to hear that. Are you sure there's no way—"

"Emily's made her decision. That's that." Mr. O'Leary frowned. "Your students are awfully noisy this morning."

Miss James twisted her head over her shoulder as far as it would go. "Quiet, children." She turned back around and rubbed the place where her neck fit into her shoulder. "I apologize, Mr. O'Leary."

"I'll inform her parents. I don't want to overwhelm you." Mr. O'Leary went away.

Miss James stared at the door like Mr. O'Leary was still standing there. She turned around slowly. "Well . . . Emily, take your seat, please. I'll get you the math work."

I kicked out my chair and sat down.

Leigh leaned over. "What happened?"

Joey picked at his alphabet strip. "Who cares? We don't need her in the concert."

Miss James' skirt swished over to my desk. I sat up so it wouldn't look like I was talking during class.

Joey kept picking at the strip, he didn't even cover it with his hand. "My dad told me so. He said, she's just making trouble for everyone just like all Jews do."

I tilted my head back like a baby bird. Miss James' eyes were big and round and blue. She looked away from me.

"Joey." Miss James dropped my math paper on my desk, it floated down like a hang glider. "I'm not going to tell you again. Leave your alphabet alone."

Miss James turned into a figure skater and spun around on her heel. She sat down at her desk and shuffled some papers so hard that a big pile slid out from under her onto the floor. I waited for her to tell me to turn around but she didn't, she just slammed her pen down and picked up the papers.

I held my pencil tight over my math work but I didn't turn around.

"Eyes forward, Emily," Miss James said in a tired voice. She hid inside her papers so I couldn't see her face. I waited, but she didn't look up.

The bell rang.

"All right, children," Miss James said. "Get your lunchtime things."

Everyone jumped up. I stuck my foot out to trip Joey.

"You too, Emily," Miss James said.

I pulled my foot back and went to get my coat. I zipped it up and tried to turn on my heel. I almost fell.

Miss James went over to the window and stared out. She breathed in so deep it made her body shake. She opened the window a crack before she let her breath out.

"Careful," I said. "You'll let the rain in."

Miss James flinched but she didn't turn around. "What'd you need, Emily?"

I took a baby step into the room. "It's raining too hard to go out."

"I know. The lunchroom teacher will find something for you to do." She pressed her nose against the glass. "Is that all?"

I nodded.

"Go, then," Miss James said. "Please." She sat down at her desk and picked up a paper from the top of the pile.

"Miss James?" I said in a little voice.

Miss James looked up. Her lips were pressed together and her forehead was tight with wrinkles.

I jumped back. "I wanna be in the Christmas concert."

"Go to lunch, Emily."

A big bolt of lightning made the room flash. I bit my lip like Mama. Miss James did not look up.

The room shook with thunder. I turned and ran down the hall before it could get me.

SIX

The girls' table was full when I got to the lunchroom. My lunchbox went clack clack clack against my leg as I looked around for someplace to sit. The only seat in the whole cafeteria was next to Joey.

I sat down on the floor between the tables.

Leigh was talking to Anna with her mouth full of peanut butter and jelly. I pulled on her arm. "Wanna trade?"

"Interrupting's rude, you know." Leigh picked up her juice box and gulped down all its insides.

I made a face and crawled under the table. A bunch of sneakers were in my face, I tried to guess who was sitting where by looking at them.

A grown-up voice said, "Emily?"

I came forward a little so I could see past Leigh's feet. A pair of fancy shoes came towards me, they were so black and shiny I could see the ceiling lights in them.

"Emily?" the voice said again, it belonged to Miss Green.

I got up.

Miss Green jumped a little. "There you are. Your daddy's waiting for you in Mr. O'Leary's office."

Leigh started to get up but I shuffled towards Miss Green and she sat down backwards. Anna pulled on her sleeve. She turned around.

I shuffled all the way to Mr. O'Leary's office, staring at my sneakers. I was a jail person going to see the judge.

As soon as we got there, Miss Green stuck her head in. "Here she is." She pulled away before the door could chop her head off. She pulled a knot out of her hair. "Go in."

My hands wanted to cross me but I didn't let them.

Daddy got up as I came in. I forgot not to be scared of him and jumped back.

"Do you know why I'm here, Emily?" Daddy said.

I shook my head and squinted at him. He had shutters closed over his brain, I couldn't read his thoughts.

"Liar." Daddy came so close he took up some of my air. "Notes home and fake signatures and meetings with the principal. You know." He breathed fire on me. I ducked. "Mr. O'Leary called me when I was in the middle of talking to a patient. He didn't want to wait, so I got interrupted. All because you can't behave. You—look at me, damn it!"

I lifted my head slowly. Daddy's whole face was on fire. He took deep accordion breaths. "I think," he said, "that you have something to say to Mr. O'Leary. And to me."

Daddy put his wolf-eyes on me to make me cooperate. Mr. O'Leary put his cloudy gray eyes on me too. They were trying to make their magic strong enough to melt me away. I screwed up my eyes so they couldn't.

"Come on, Emily," Daddy said. "We're waiting."

"Yes, please, Emily." Mr. O'Leary sat down on the edge of his desk. "You still want to be in the concert, don't you?"

I watched my shoe go around and around on the floor while I tried again to remember what I did wrong.

Mr. O'Leary turned towards Daddy. "Stubborn, isn't she?"

Daddy's shoulders fell down like they were sad. "Mr. O'Leary, I don't—" His cell phone played his and Mama's special song. "Excuse me."

Daddy pulled his phone out so hard his pocket ripped. "Hey, babe, I'll call you back, OK?" He squeezed the phone tight. "What? Are you all right?"

Daddy walked out of Mr. O'Leary's office. I stretched my hearing as far as it would go, but he was too far away already.

Mr. O'Leary cleared his throat. "Well, Emily, your daddy's pretty upset. Is it worth it?"

I watched my feet kicking my chair while I tried to think of something to say.

Daddy came back in the room. "I'm afraid I have to run. My wife blew out her tire . . . she's stranded with our son."

"I understand." Mr. O'Leary adjusted his tie. "I could excuse Emily for the day if you'd like."

"No. Thank you. It's just a blown tire." Daddy zipped his coat up tight. "You know, my kid's the only one who doesn't celebrate Christmas. It would be nice if she could at least participate in the concert like everyone else."

Mr. O'Leary's jaw tightened. "I'm sorry about your wife's accident."

Daddy stared at Mr. O'Leary while he put on his gloves. "Thank you," he said, and turned away.

"Bye, Daddy." I stood on my tiptoes to kiss Daddy's cheek.

Daddy sighed. "Emily. Do me a favor and be good for the rest of the day, will you?"

I nodded but Daddy was already leaving, he didn't see.

It was raining even harder by the time school ended. Water dripped down the windows, everything was bent out of shape again. I squinted, but it didn't change anything.

"Get your things, Emily," Miss James said. I waited for her to go away, but she didn't. "Are you squinting because you can't see well?"

I erased fog off the window with my hand and shook my head.

I could feel Miss James watching me. I turned around. Her head was all the way down on her shoulder like it was too heavy for her neck to hold up anymore.

A question rose up inside me. I pressed in my stomach. “Miss James?”

“Yes, Emily, what is it?”

“What’s autism?”

Miss James pulled out the chair from my desk. It was way too little for her, the sides dug into her thighs. She got up again and sat on the desk instead.

“Well,” Miss James said. “That is a difficult question, Emily. Is there a special reason you want to know?”

I pressed my stomach in tighter. “Alex has it.”

“You need to talk a little less softly.” Miss James squeezed her hands together. “I can’t hear you.”

On the other side of the room, Joey knocked into a chair and made it fall over.

Miss James slid off the desk. “If you’re ready, children, wait for me by the door. I will be there in a second.”

I put my hands over my ears to get Miss James’ words out of my head. She was saying something in a soft voice, I took my hands away again. She smiled at me. “Hurry and get your things.”

I turned and walked slowly towards my cubby.

“Emily,” Miss James said. “We’ll talk tomorrow.”

I tossed my hair over my shoulder and kept going like I didn’t hear her.

I didn’t see Mama or Daddy anywhere when we got outside. Cars were lined up everywhere, I put my hand on top of my eyes to see better.

Leigh tugged on my sleeve. “Let’s walk.” She ran off towards home. I turned around and looked to see if anyone was coming for us. My heart was beating too fast, I opened my raincoat to make sure I could breathe.

Someone shoved me from behind. I slid all the way to the curb.

I got up slowly and stared down at my shirt. My unicorn's hair was all full of mud, its horn looked like a million people stepped on it. I tried to wipe the mud off but it was half made out of glue, it wouldn't wipe.

Joey came down the hill towards me, his eyes were little and full of meanness. "That's what you get for ruining the Christmas concert," he said. "Want some more?"

I scraped a big gob of mud off my shirt and threw it at him.

A car honked just then. I started to run towards it, then I saw it wasn't Mama's. Hers is shiny and new and the color of the sky. This car was an ugly peeling brown. It looked like it was borrowed from the war.

A man got out of the car. He was short and thin like a skeleton. "Joey. Over here."

Joey turned red. Mud slid through his fingers and melted into the ground.

"I'm telling," I said.

Joey ran after me. "My dad won't want to see your ugly face," he said between breaths. "He'll punch you dead."

I ignored him. There was no such thing and anyway, I could run faster than any skeleton.

Joey was all the way at the top of the hill when I got to the car. It felt hot as summer even though rain was falling all around me. I stared at Joey's dad to get his spell off me.

"What are you supposed to be?" Joey's dad said.

"Joey pushed me in the mud for no reason," I said.

Joey's dad looked me up and down. His eyes twinkled like black ice. "No reason, huh? I can think of several."

My throat felt tight. I twisted my head over my shoulder to see if Miss James was coming out of the school. She wasn't.

A dragon was huffing and puffing behind me, Joey was coming. I made my hand into a fist and filled it with pretend mud.

Joey started to say something. His dad play-punched him on the shoulder. "Hey Joe, I hear you're picking on girls now. What gives?"

Joey's eyes were bright with meanness. "That's a girl? I thought it was just a big, stupid Jew." His voice echoed over the wind and got stuck in my ears.

All the grown-ups on the sidewalk stopped what they were doing and stared.

Joey's dad pulled the car door open. "Get in."

Joey tumbled into the car. His dad twisted his head over his shoulder and stared back at the other grown-ups. He looked like a mouse trying to get away from a cat.

The mouse looked at me. His eyes weren't working right, they went right through me like I was a ghost. "Sorry he said that." He slid back into the car and started the engine. "Hurry up and get that goddamn seatbelt on, will you?"

Joey let the seatbelt fall out of his hands. His cheeks turned pink.

Joey's dad pulled away from the curb very fast.

The rain started to come down harder. I looked down the street, but in all those grown-ups, there was no one I knew. Leigh was long gone and Mama had never come. Even Uncle Max forgot me.

My eyes burned me. I rubbed them with the back of my sleeve. It was the only part of me that wasn't all muddy. I tried to get a thought-message to Patrick to tell him I had to walk, but the rain was in the way, I couldn't get through.

"My mom's gonna be so mad when she sees me," I said, as if Leigh was here. But I knew she wasn't. I couldn't even pretend.

I wiped my eyes and walked slowly home, hoping the rain would wipe away all the mud before Mama opened the door. The wind roared loud in my ears. On the street, cars zoomed through big puddles and splashed me all over.

I was almost home when a yellow car pulled over. A man rolled down the window. "You look all wet," he said. "Want a ride?"

My heart beat fast. I wanted to run across the street but then the bad stranger would know where I lived. "No thank you," I said. I turned and walked in the other direction so he couldn't trap me while I crossed.

The bad man drove away. I ran across the street without looking. I didn't stop 'til I was at my house. I banged and banged on the door.

No one answered.

I held the doorbell in. Mama came down from her room, she thumped and shaked like an earthquake. She pulled the door open hard. "What?" Her back got less stiff and she remembered to put on her smile. "Oh. Emily. Come in."

I took a baby step into the house. Mama's eyes got big and wide. "What the hell happened to you?"

I wiped my boots as fast as I could. "It's not my fault, Mama. Joey shoved me and then—"

"Go take a bath. Daddy's on his way home with Uncle Max."

I stopped in the middle of taking off my coat. "Uncle Max's coming over?"

Mama's jaw twitched. "Close that door. You're letting the cold in."

I closed the door.

"Hurry up with that bath," Mama said. "The sooner you're finished, the sooner I can let you help me with dinner." She smiled. She was like the old Mama before Alex caught autism only her smile didn't fit her anymore, even her nice words sounded sad.

I put my raincoat carefully on its hook. "I'll take a very fast bath, Mama."

"As long as you're clean," Mama said, and smiled another smile that was too big for her face.

I dropped my gloves on the floor. "Where's Alex, anyway?"

"With Daddy." Mama's voice was very soft. She lifted her head. "Start your bath already, will you?"

Mama went in the kitchen. Her bathrobe belt was dragging on the floor, she was wearing her early-morning robe when it was almost time for dinner.

I ran up the steps into the bathroom. I turned the hot water on as far as it would go cause my bath is always cold. Then I turned into a spy and went into Alex's room.

Alex's crib was empty.

I checked my bath but it wasn't hot yet. I sneaked into Mama's room next.

The room was big and full of empty space. Mama's half of the bed was all messed up.

I felt like Mama was in the room watching me even though I knew she was downstairs. There was a little bottle of pills on her table, the label said a long name I couldn't read. I picked them up and shook them. The steps creaked, I put the bottle back.

I meant to walk away, but my feet ran.

I locked the bathroom door tight. Then I pulled my clothes off and jumped in the bath like it was a swimming pool.

The steps shook, an angry sea god came upstairs. "Emily? Are you all right?"

"I'm in the bath, Mama."

Mama rattled the doorknob. "Still?"

I rubbed soap in my hair as fast as I could. When I was all done with the bath, I dried myself off and put on my dirty clothes again so I would be done quicker.

"Don't you ever lock the door when you're in the bath again," Mama said.

"Why?" I pretended to be looking for a comb so I could get away from Mama's eyes.

"What if you fall?" Mama looked me up and down. "Emily, those clothes are filthy."

"I know. I—"

"Well, change them, then."

I jumped back. "But you said to hurry."

"What?"

The front door squeaked open. "Bec?" Daddy called.

Mama hurried to the steps. "Be down in a second." She twisted her head around and mouthed, "Go change." I pretended not to know what she was saying as I followed her down the steps.

Daddy was hiding in the kitchen, Mama slid in there with him. Uncle Max was sitting on the couch.

Alex was on his lap.

I jumped off the bottom step. "Alex's eyes look like dirty glass."

Uncle Max flinched. "Only from far away," he said. "Come hold him and you'll see."

"I don't wanna."

"You sure? I'll show you a secret."

I took a tiny little step closer.

"Watch this," Uncle Max said. "Alex hates being touched. So—"

My hand wanted to slap Alex's face. I told it not to but it wouldn't listen. Alex whimpered as it came towards him.

Uncle Max slid back a little. "You're moving way too fast. Don't scare him like that."

I glared at Alex but it didn't make one dent in the force field between me and Uncle Max. "Why are you such a scaredy-cat?"

Uncle Max looked me up and down. I didn't mind cause his eyes weren't mean. "What happened to you?" he said.

"Nothing."

"No. Come here." Uncle Max reached towards me.

"I wanna sit on your lap," I said in a baby voice.

"Come on up, then." Uncle Max patted his other knee. "There's room enough for both of you."

I climbed up and stared into Alex's eyes. He made a funny noise and turned his head away.

Uncle Max rubbed my back. I tried to ignore him but his spell worked, the angry thing in my throat turned into a ball of tears. I blinked and breathed deep to keep them inside me but they wouldn't stay.

"That's right," Uncle Max said. "Get it all out."

My eyes ran out of tears before I ran out of sadness, I cried even though nothing came out. I leaned against Uncle Max and waited for him to say something, but he didn't.

"A bad man tried to give me a ride," I said.

"Oh?" Uncle Max said. Alex made his weird half-cry again, Uncle Max sat up straighter. "Anything else happen?" His voice was soft as pillows. I put my head closer against him.

Mama came in just then. She put her hands on her hips and stared at us, her eyes took a picture but it wasn't a nice one. "Dinner's ready," she said.

"We'll be there in a minute," Uncle Max said.

Mama leaned over, so close he ducked. "Now," she said, and picked Alex up like he was a strawberry.

Alex turned stiff as a board in her hands.

"Aren't we going to do candles?" I said.

Mama bit her lip. "Ask your father. That's his department." She turned and walked away.

Uncle Max tapped his fingers on his elbow. "So," he said. "What else is new?"

"Nothing," I said. But Uncle Max had a not-believing look in his eyes.

Mama called, "Maxwell. Emily." and made my thoughts fall apart.

Daddy looked up as I came in the dining room. "You're filthy. Go change." Mama came out of the kitchen with a big plate of something. Daddy blocked it with his hand. "We can't eat yet. Emily's too dirty."

"She had a bath, Dan," Mama said. Daddy kept his arm in the way for a second, then he slapped it on his thigh.

I hopped up and down on one foot as Mama put pot roast on everyone's plate. "Aren't we gonna do candles?"

Daddy looked at Mama. "We have company," he said.

Uncle Max pushed his chair away from the table. "Oh, I don't mind."

"Yeah, well . . ." Daddy breathed deep. "I think we'll skip it, anyway."

I squeezed the top of my chair as hard as I could before I sat down.

Daddy reached across the table and grabbed my plate.

"Hey!" I said.

"People with dirty shirts do not get fed."

I looked at Uncle Max. He was staring into the plate like he was searching for buried treasure. His fork went tap tap tap and his leg shook under the table where he thought I couldn't see it.

I tried Mama instead. She tried to smile but her smile wouldn't come all the way onto her face. "Hurry up so your food doesn't get cold," she said.

I pushed my chair out and got up as fast as I could. It crashed to the floor. Mama flinched, Alex whimpered. Uncle Max didn't look up, not even for a second. He clutched his fork more tightly and moved his lips like he was saying a secret prayer.

I glared at Alex. "Wanna come, scaredy-cat?" Daddy started to get up. I ran out of the room and upstairs before he could do anything to me.

In my room, I pulled my shirt off and threw it hard as I could. It hit the wall. My undershirt was dirty too. I ripped it off even though Daddy didn't know about it.

The shirts were all huddled together in the drawer to keep themselves warm. I closed the drawer and opened the closet instead. I pulled a sweater off the hanger so hard that that hanger tube came out of its socket and all the sweaters fell on the floor.

I picked up a sweater and backed away. I closed the closet slowly and quietly like I was in the library.

I was putting the sweater over my head when Daddy came in. I turned around without pulling it down.

Daddy looked all blue like the sweater. "What happened in here?" he said.

"Nothing." The air tasted like wool. I pulled the sweater all the way down. "The hanger thing broke in the closet."

Daddy pulled the closet open. I tiptoed behind him to look over his shoulder.

"Go downstairs," Daddy said.

I put two fingers in my mouth. "I wanna help you fix it."

"Not now." Daddy slammed the closet closed. I pulled my fingers out of my mouth before he could turn around. "Dinner's getting cold."

I backed out of the room and waited by the steps for Daddy.

Uncle Max looked up as I came into the dining room. "Nice sweater," he said. I smiled wide and thanked him, but the Thank You got lost in Daddy scraping his chair against the floor.

Uncle Max stared into the empty menorah like there were invisible candles there. "Dan?"

Daddy looked up. "We'll talk after dinner. Eat."

Uncle Max sighed and cocked his head like a parrot. He smiled at me, but his eyes looked dark and sad. "How was school today, Emily?"

Mama dropped her fork. "School's going really well for Emily. She got all Excellents on her first report card last month, and she really loves her teacher."

Uncle Max turned slowly towards Mama. "That's great, Bec. Really. But I was talking to Emily."

Mama bit her lip. "Pass me the juice, please, Dan." She grabbed the container out of Daddy's hands and started pouring. Her hands shook but someone must have had a secret magic cause she didn't spill.

"Don't stare, Emily," Mama said. I watched Uncle Max brush crumbs off the table instead.

"So how was it?" Uncle Max said.

I looked at Mama but she was busy with the juice, I was safe. "Not so good."

"Why not?"

I picked at the tablecloth. "Cause—"

Daddy grabbed my wrist. "Don't do that," he said, he turned into a snake and hissed it.

"Dan," Uncle Max said as I rubbed my wrist.

"Not until after dinner." Daddy's eyes shot super torpedoes. "Everyone eat."

I stared at my plate. The pot roast and the vegetables didn't like each other, they kept trying to move away but the sauce made them come together again. I pushed at them with my fork until Daddy said, "Emily."

Uncle Max dropped his spoon. "Damn it, Dan, you're gonna have to listen to me," he said. Daddy started to say something but Uncle Max said, "No more waiting. We talk now."

I looked back and forth from Daddy to Uncle Max. Daddy's lips were pressed tight together like a wooden soldier's and Uncle Max's eyes looked like two oil wells on fire. I looked away.

"Go ahead," Daddy said through his closed-up lips.

Uncle Max sighed. "You know, Dan, you used to make my sister happy. Now she's not. In fact, I don't think any of you are."

Mama twisted a lock of hair around her finger. "Don't worry about us, Maxwell. Please. We're fine. We're just . . ." Her voice faded away to nothing like it was out of batteries.

Uncle Max stared at Mama. She turned away so he couldn't see her thoughts.

"Oh, Bec," Uncle Max said. "Haven't you learned anything from all my mess-ups?" He squeezed the back of his chair. "You can't keep ignoring everything that's wrong in your life. You can't keep ignoring this."

Mama twisted her napkin over and over. It broke apart and made a mess on the table. "I-I'm not. I'm—"

"Don't rip your napkin," I said in a loud voice.

Uncle Max glanced at me. "You are, Bec," he said. "You're running from doctor to doctor with Alex looking for someone who'll tell you what you want to hear and in the meantime, look what it's doing to Emily." Uncle Max's voice got softer still, I had to turn the volume all the way up on my ears to hear him. "She needs you, Bec, every bit as much as Alex does."

Mama looked at me. I squeezed my eyes shut and tried to turn into a snowflake, but I couldn't melt away.

Uncle Max reached across the table and took Mama's hand. "You gotta stop this. Alex is what he is and no Maxer how much you wish . . ." He shook his head. "For everyone's sake, please stop."

No one said anything for a long time. Instead they sat frozen like they were in a picture.

"Well," I said, and pushed my plate away. I wanted to hear my voice so I knew I wasn't deaf.

Alex shrieked once and stopped. Mama jumped up and rubbed his back but he made himself stiff. She dropped her hand again and stared at him.

Uncle Max leaned over Mama's plate. "Are there any classes for parents of autistic children at your hospital, Dan? Maybe you and Bec—"

"We're fine." Daddy still didn't move his mouth. I tried to say something without moving mine but it came out all mumbly.

Daddy turned towards me. "Stop making silly noises and help Mama clear the table."

I picked up my plate. "Come on, pot roast. Let me show you your new home." I put the whole plate in the refrigerator instead of putting my leftovers in a container like I'm supposed to. Cold air came out. I closed the door but the cold wouldn't go back where it belonged.

I tiptoed back into the dining room.

"She's gonna end up like me," Uncle Max said.

"What's wrong with being like you?" I said.

Uncle Max got up slowly, he was older than old all of a sudden. He kneeled down and adjusted my collar. "That's a complicated question, kiddo."

Mama was putting her angry face on, her lips were tight and her back was getting stiff. Uncle Max ignored her. "Before you were born, I did some things I wasn't too proud of. I used to—"

"That was then," Mama said. "You don't do those things anymore, do you?"

"No," Uncle Max said. "I don't."

"Well, then why even talk about them?"

"Because," Uncle Max said to the floor. His voice was so soft even it couldn't hear him. He looked up at me again. His eyes were wide and round and very black. "I'm sorry, Emily. I don't think I can explain this to you right now."

Uncle Max held onto my collar. I wanted to hug him but I couldn't reach, instead I put my hand on top of his. Uncle Max patted it before he let me go.

"Emily," Mama said. "Go get the dessert plates."

I backwards-walked to the kitchen and climbed on the counter to get the plates. Mama didn't come in and catch me.

When I finished putting the plates on the table, Uncle Max said, "Come see this cake I bought." I tiptoed up to him, he put his hand on my shoulder. His cake was nothing special, it was just a big white circle.

"This is a starting over cake." Uncle Max looked over at Mama. "We're agreed, right?"

Mama looked down at her hands. "Give us a few days to think it over."

"Think what over?" I said.

Uncle Max threw the cake-cutting thing on the table, it clanged loud and erased my voice. I backed away to my seat.

"Damn it, haven't you guys been listening?" Uncle Max said. "I'm giving you a way out. Don't you get that?" He picked up the cake-cutting thing. "Forget it. Let's eat." He tossed cake on his plate.

Mama squeezed Uncle Max's shoulder, he made his back stiff like Alex's.

I picked up my fork and tapped it against the side of my plate. "Autism, autism, autism," I sang.

Daddy grabbed my wrist.

"What did you say?" Mama pushed her hair behind her ear.

I tried to slide down in my seat but Daddy wouldn't let me. "I was just singing to Alex."

Mama sighed deep. "Go do your homework."

Uncle Max smiled and gave me a thumbs-up as I got up, but I knew he was sad. I watched him as I backwards-walked out of the room. He didn't turn back to Mama 'til I was gone.

I got my homework things out of my backpack and put them on the coffee table. I kneeled down, my knees moaned and groaned. I ignored them.

The math homework had a drawing of a bunch of balloons. "Put these balloons in groups of two," it said.

In the dining room, Mama said, "Give us time."

I separated the balloons into three groups of two. "How many groups?" the homework asked, and I wrote the number three.

Uncle Max said, "It's for the best, Bec, it really is."

The homework ditto said, "What is 3 x 2?"

In the dining room, someone's fork scraped against their plate.

Alex started to cry and stopped again.
A big clap of thunder almost broke the sky in half.
I picked up my pencil and slowly wrote my answer.

SEVEN

It was snowing in the lunchroom. I asked Leigh about it but the wind roared loud and erased what I was saying. Miss James walked by with a stack of papers and Joey made his slushball invisible. She said something to me, but the wind roared and roared.

The loudspeaker buzzed and chased the wind away. I walked and walked and walked. A light covered Mr. O'Leary's door. It attacked my eyes. I wanted to look away but I couldn't even though it was making me not breathe. I couldn't even move.

I gasped and gasped and gasped but instead of my breath, my heartbeat kept coming out of me. I tried to talk to the light in my thoughts, I said I'm sorry, I'm sorry, I'm sorry.

The light let me go. I opened my eyes and was in my room. Outside the window, the rain went drip drip drip. I sat straight up and rubbed my lungs to make sure the dream wasn't in them.

It was too dark as I tiptoed downstairs. But in the dining room, all the lights were on. They gave me a headache even though I tried not to look.

There were dishes and coffee cups lying all over the table. I sniffed a cup to make sure it wasn't poisoned before I took the dishes into the kitchen. My body was tired but I didn't want to go back to sleep. Instead I sat swinging my legs and waiting for Mama.

I turned to look at the clock and saw a little box on the table. I picked it up and turned it over. There was an envelope hiding under the box, it had my name on it in tiny letters that ran together like they were trying to be fancy and didn't know how.

Elephant steps came from upstairs. "Emily," Mama said. "What are you doing up?"

I pushed the box away. "I couldn't sleep."

"Well, it's not morning yet. Go back upstairs. And leave that alone until later."

"Where'd it come from?"

"This weather is terrible. I'm sure you'll have a snow day."

"A snow day?" I said, I was talking to myself but my voice came out loud. "But it's raining."

"It's freezing rain, Emily. Go back to bed."

I stuffed the box into my pocket and went to my room. Patrick was still sleeping, he roared when I picked him up. I waited 'til he settled down before I tore off the wrapping paper.

Under the paper, the box was all velvet and soft like a cat. I opened it slowly and looked in.

A gold necklace lay asleep in the box. It was wearing a Jewish star with a Hebrew letter in it. I poked Patrick and held the necklace out in front of his trunk. The Jewish star spun around and around. When it got dizzy, I put the necklace away and opened the envelope.

A folded up paper fell onto the bed. I opened it slowly and put it where Patrick could see.

Dear Emily,

Every little girl should get a Chanukah present, no Maxer what her mom and dad have to say about it. The necklace is for when you're all grown up, but I wanted you to have it now so you'd know how special you are.

About the question you asked me: that's gonna have to wait 'til you're grown up too. But for now—

Mama came in just then. I dropped the letter, a key fell off it and landed on the bed. I scooped the key up and stuffed in my sock.

Mama squeezed the doorknob. "I said not to open that yet."

"Ssh. The necklace is sleeping."

Mama rolled her eyes. "A necklace? Let me see it."

I hugged the box tight. "Patrick won't let me show you."

Mama's eyes got wide. She breathed so deep her whole body shook. "No school today. Go back to bed." She went down the hall.

I pulled the covers tight around me and listened to the rain tap tap tapping on the window. I closed my eyes, Patrick played a sad note with his trunk. I held him tight but the wind still shook the house.

Alex made a half-cry and Mama thumped down the hall in time with the rain. I slid over to the wall and made baby noises. Alex just cried louder.

I sat up quick when Mama came in my room again.

"You're awake. Good. Get dressed," Mama said.

I hugged Patrick tighter than tight. "You said there's no school today."

"There's not." Mama looked out the window at the rain, but it didn't change. She pulled the curtains closed. "I'm taking you and Alex for a ride."

My chest felt tight. I stared at Mama. She leaned Alex on her arms and stared out the window like she didn't remember that the curtains were closed.

"Mama?" I put my hand under my shirt. "What does Miss James do when there's no school?"

"Get dressed already, Emily."

I put on my sweater. "Where are we going?"

"Hon?" Daddy called.

"Coming, Dan." Mama hurried out of the room. She looked littler than me.

I slid out sideways and followed her.

Mama and Daddy's door was closed. I made myself flat against it.

"You're taking her out of school for this?" Daddy said.

"Oh, she won't mind," Mama answered. "I told her it was a snow day."

I gasped.

Daddy said, "In this weather? Wasn't what happened yesterday bad enough?"

"I'll be fine, Dan."

"You're taking too many chances. What good is any of this going to do if you and Alex wind up dead?"

Daddy's words went through me like Cupid's arrows. I shivered but they wouldn't get out of me. I ran into the bathroom and locked the door and pulled down my pants so I could sit on the toilet.

Mama came out of her room. Her feet were angry, they went stomp stomp stomp away from me. "Emily?" she called. She used her nice voice but it didn't fool me.

I slid slowly off the toilet and came out into the hall.

Daddy was coming out of the room with a towel over his shoulder. My heart beat faster than fast. "Daddy?"

Daddy turned around.

I opened and closed my mouth like a fish. "I wanna go to school."

"I need to get in there." Daddy slid past me. I jumped out of the way before he could bump me.

I turned and walked away. Mama was kneeling on the laundry box halfway between the bathroom and my room. I tried to see her reflection in the window but it wasn't dark enough, all I saw was rain streaking down like God was crying.

I went downstairs. After a long time Mama came in with Alex. She put him in his high chair and said, "Are you hungry?"

I knew she wasn't talking to me. "I'm starving."

Mama twisted her head over her shoulder. "Do me a favor and get me the milk. A banana too."

I pulled a banana off the bunch so hard it ripped open. Mama cut it up and threw it into a bowl of cereal. "Here," she said. "Eat."

I kicked my chair out and picked up my spoon. I was a treasure hunter, I dug through the cereal looking for gold. I didn't find any. The cereal turned back into cereal and let me eat it.

Daddy came downstairs. Mama froze in the middle of feeding Alex. She turned and stared at him.

"Going to work?" Mama said.

"Nah." Daddy pulled at the middle of his shirt like he was straightening an invisible tie. "I don't want to risk it in this weather." He looked straight at Mama. "Your plans?"

Mama looked away. "Well . . ."

"Well what?"

"Well, nothing."

Daddy went to the refrigerator. "Let's not start this again, Rebekah." He took a pan out and cracked two eggs into it. "Still want to look at schools for Alex?"

"Of course."

"Good." Daddy stirred the eggs. "I'll come with you."

Mama turned her fire-eyes all the way up. I ducked under the table and crawled towards Alex, I kept my eye on Mama's feet to make sure she wasn't coming near us.

"Fine," Mama said. "Whatever."

I stuck my head out to see what was going on.

"Get out from under there." Daddy turned back around. "Give me your keys, Bec."

"I can drive, Dan."

"Of course you—"

"Like I care. Here." Mama banged the keys down on the table.

Daddy stared at the keys like he was trying to read a secret code. He sighed deep as the wind and went out to start the car.

Mama turned on me and Alex. "You heard Daddy. Get up."

The car engine vibrated through me. I slid out from under the table. "You're scaring Alex, Mama."

Mama looked at Alex. He had his head scrunched down into the high chair tray, he was talking to it in baby language.

"I'm sorry." Mama pushed past me. Alex sat up and pointed at something in the ceiling.

"How come Alex doesn't know how to walk?" I asked.

Mama pulled down the high chair tray too fast. It made a cracking sound. "Dammit." She twisted her head over her shoulder. "Go wait in the car, Emily. Please."

"But—"

Mama's eyes were wide as lakes as she turned towards me. "Alex does know how to walk. I like to carry him sometimes, that's all. Now please . . . no more questions. Let's just go." She pushed the door open and went out. It swung closed, I watched it cut into the sky.

I got on my knees and crawled to the door, I was a baby too little to walk. I couldn't open it from the floor, I had to turn back into a little girl. I shoved the door open and ran outside.

There was ice hiding under the rain. My feet slid away from me and I went down, down, down all the way to the driveway. My eyes burned me but I didn't let them cry. My knees burned me too. I got up slowly and brushed them off.

Mama jumped out of the car. "Dan, look at her. She—"

"I saw." Daddy came out slowly like he was afraid the rain would get him too. "You know better than to run in this kind of weather, Emily."

"I was just—"

"Roll up your pants."

I did. My knee was all red, little pieces of white skin hung off it like spider webs. I squeezed my eyes shut so I wouldn't have to keep looking at it.

Daddy tugged at my pants. "Get in," he said. I held onto the car until I was in the back seat.

"It's just a skinned knee," Daddy said to Mama. "She'll live."

The car crawled backwards out of the driveway. No one said anything. I watched the rain fall and fall and fall while Mama played with the radio and Alex slept.

"Where are we going?" I said. No one answered.

The car tilted down the parkway entrance. I held on tight to the door.

When we were going straight again, Mama said, "I'm sorry."

Daddy patted her hand and said, "I know." He grabbed the steering wheel again.

"Why are you sorry?" I asked.

Mama looked at Daddy. "It's complicated. It's . . . oh, why am I explaining this to you? It's a grown-up Maxer."

My cheeks felt tight. I opened the window to get fresh air in my nose.

"It's cold out," Mama said. "Close that." I ignored her.

Daddy's cell phone rang. "Hello? No, we decided to keep Emily out of school today. Weather. No, of course it has nothing to do with your decision regarding her—"

A big truck tried to jump in front of us. Daddy pushed the brakes all the way to the floor. The car started to slide. I grabbed the door so tight my fingers hurt. In front of me, Mama did the same thing.

Somehow Daddy made us stop sliding.

"Listen," he said. "Can I call you back?" He hung up. "We're all right."

"No more using the phone while you're driving," Mama said. "Please."

Daddy patted her hand again. "I won't." After a minute he added, "That was Mr. O'Leary. He was concerned about Emily's absence."

Daddy gave Mama a look, but she shrugged.

"He was afraid we were retaliating for the concert," Daddy said.

Mama twisted a knob on the radio. It blasted loud. "Who cares about the stupid concert?" she said, and turned it back. "The whole thing's a pain in the neck anyway."

"I know you feel that way. But for Emily to be the only one not participating . . ."

"Well, that's what she gets for us staying Jewish. I wish we hadn't." Mama closed the window. "Emily, I said it's too cold in here."

My stomach felt tighter than tight. I felt for the window button but I couldn't find it.

I coughed. The cough got harder and turned into throw-up.

"God damn it!" Daddy pulled off the parkway. "You just had to throw up all over yourself, didn't you?"

I sniffed. "I couldn't help it."

Daddy was already getting out of the car. "I don't suppose you thought to bring a change of clothes for her," he said to Mama. She shook her head.

"Well . . ." Daddy stared at me. "I guess I'll take her to a gas station and see if I can get her cleaned up."

Mama shrugged.

Daddy straightened up fast. "What?"

Mama played with the radio knob. "We're gonna be late."

"We can't exactly take her like this, can we?" Daddy wiped his forehead with his sleeve. "There's gotta be a station nearby. This is an exit ramp, after all. Come on, Emily."

Cars were passing on my side, they were going fast and making water splash up. I wanted to crouch down but Daddy had his impatient face on. I squeezed my eyes shut as I got out in case a car hitted me.

Daddy grabbed my hand. He walked so fast I had to put my feet on superspeed to keep up. We went across a big street and down the block and across a little street.

Daddy asked the gas station man for the bathroom key. The gas station man blinked at him like he was just waking up. He said something I couldn't hear.

"No," Daddy said. "I am not buying gas." He shoved me forward. "My daughter's sick, see. I have to—"

The gas station man walked away. He acted like he was straightening some candies on a shelf, but he was only pretending.

Daddy tapped his fingers on the counter.

The gas station man came back. "You buy gas or no?"

"Listen, you idiot." Daddy pushed me forward some more. I almost fell. "She threw up."

"You buy gas or you leave. No gas, no bathroom. Sorry."

Daddy grabbed my hand too tight and dragged me back to the car. He flung the door open. "We're going home."

"No, Dan. Alex—"

Daddy leaned over Mama. His eyes were shiny and mad like a wolf's. "I said we're going home. Cancel Alex's appointment." He got in and slammed the door.

We were almost all the way home when Mama said, "Dan?"

Daddy squinted into the windshield. "What is it?"

Mama twisted her hair around her finger. "Never mind."

"Look." Daddy squeezed the steering wheel tight. "Alex doesn't need preschool yet. When the weather's better, we'll—"

"I wanted to do it now." Mama looked down at the floor. "He needs stimulation, Dan."

Daddy was coming fast towards a red light. He hit the brakes hard. "It'll just have to wait."

Mama twisted the knob on the radio the whole rest of the way home.

When we got in the driveway, Daddy said, "Go change, Emily. I'll take you to school." He got out. Mama stayed sitting in the car.

I followed Daddy down the path. "Daddy?"

"Huh?" Daddy jiggled his key in the lock.

"How come Alex has autism?"

Daddy looked at me over his shoulder. "He just does. Come on."

I went inside. Daddy went the other way to ask Mama if she was all right. I shivered as I headed for the steps.

Daddy came back in. "Emily," he said, "put your dirty clothes in a bag for Mama to wash, OK?"

I ran up the steps. I could hear Mama moving around downstairs, she was like an earthquake. I pulled my clothes off carefully and folded them up. Then I wrapped myself in my blanket and took my temperature with a pretend thermometer.

Mama came up and opened my door without knocking. I wrapped myself tighter in the blanket so she wouldn't see me.

"Emily, did you find—" Mama x-rayed me with her eyes. "What in the world?"

I rolled over and stared at the wall. "I'm sick." I made myself as stiff as I could. "I caught autism from Alex."

I could feel Mama staring at me. After a long time she sighed. "I guess maybe we should talk." She sat down at the edge of the bed.

I sat up. "Mama?"

Mama's head drooped down like it was too heavy for her. I hugged Patrick tight against me so he wouldn't see.

"It's OK, Mama," I said.

Mama patted my hand under the blanket. She smiled. Her smile was almost real.

"Come on," Mama said. "Get dressed." She got up and walked away.

I shivered and turned Patrick around so he wouldn't see me without clothes on.

When I got downstairs, Mama and Daddy were talking in whisper language. I tiptoed towards them. "I'm ready."

Daddy cleared his throat. "Emily. Before we go, Mama and I would like to talk to you."

My heart beat faster than fast. I kicked my chair out like I didn't care. "About what?"

"You know we're looking at special schools for Alex."

I stared at the clock on top of the sink and tried to guess what time it said. Daddy waved his hand in front of my face. "I'm talking to you, Emily. Pay attention." I jerked awake. "That's better. Now, as I was saying . . . Mama thought . . . that is, Mama and I thought you'd like to go to a special school too."

Daddy was smiling. I knew he wanted me too smile too but my mouth wouldn't let me. I wiggled and squirmed. "What about Miss James?"

"What about her?"

I stared down at my shoes. "Well, she can't come teach at the special school, can she?"

Daddy looked over his shoulder at Mama. "Don't worry about that." He smiled again. His smile felt like a lie. "I know you'll like your new teachers even better than Miss James."

I watched my feet kicking my chair. My thoughts were all tangled up in each other, none of them could get on my tongue.

"You'll love it, Emily," Mama said. "You'll make new friends and learn a lot more. And best of all, we'll never have to worry about Christmas concerts again." Mama wiped fog off the window. "All we have to do is wait until this weather clears up," she said. Her voice was little and soft like it came from somewhere inside the clouds.

"So we're decided," Daddy said. "The next clear day we get, we'll look—"

"I told you: I already know which school," Mama said.

Daddy glanced at her. "I think it's too far. Let's drive out there before we commit to anything."

Mama wilted like a dried-up flower. She stared at the table and tapped her foot.

Daddy sighed. "Emily, get your school things together, OK?"

I kept my eye on Mama as I got off my chair. She sat frozen in place like a statue. I skipped to the hallway. Mama didn't move one inch.

It was quiet as I pulled my coat off its hook and shoved my arms into the sleeves. In the kitchen, Mama and Daddy talked in low voices. The rain tap-danced on the window.

As I zipped my coat up tight, Alex shrieked from somewhere far away.

I could barely hear him over the roar of the wind.

EIGHT

Daddy was on his phone when I went out to the car. I put my hand on the door handle and tried to hear. He waved at the lock to tell me the car was open.

I crawled inside.

"If you have time for this conversation, you have time to see me in person," Daddy said. I grabbed my seatbelt but there was something dried up on it. I slid towards the other seat.

Daddy twisted his head over his shoulder. "Emily, what are you doing? Hurry up and get your seatbelt on." He turned back around before I could answer. "Yes. I'm leaving now."

Daddy flipped the phone closed and started the car. He backed out way too fast and raced to the school like he was afraid the rain would get us.

The school looked dark and empty as Daddy pulled up. I stared at the floor so I wouldn't have to see it. There was an empty candy wrapper half buried under the seat, it was a Golden Ticket. I tried to grab it but I couldn't cause my seatbelt was in the way. I twisted against it to try to get free.

Daddy leaned over me. "Come on." I watched the belt slide back into its hole.

The rain made everything slippery. I wanted to hold Daddy's had but he was already walking away. Instead I shuffled up the steps, I watched my shoes getting wet.

Daddy knocked hard on the door. It opened so fast we almost fell back.

Mr. O'Leary was on the other side.

"There you are," he said. "Run along to Miss James' room, Emily."

Daddy started to follow Mr. O'Leary down the hall. I tiptoed behind them.

"I'm afraid I only have about two minutes to give you," Mr. O'Leary said.

I tiptoed closer but my shoelace clicked on the floor and gave me away.

Daddy turned around. "Emily, you heard Mr. O'Leary. Go to your classroom."

I flipped my hair over my shoulder and walked down the hall. Everyone was bunched up at the door. Miss James smiled at me but I wasn't sure if her smile was real or not, she stared at me and squeezed her hands together.

"Oh, Emily," Miss James said. "Hi. I'm glad you could make it."

"I'm not," Joey said.

Miss James made her lips thin and tight. Her Mama face bounced off Joey and made me scrunch down.

"Well, uh, we were getting ready to go to the music room," Miss James said. "You can come watch, I guess, or, uh, you could sit in Mrs. Bell's room and read a book."

"Don't worry," I said. "I can be in the concert too." Jiminy Cricket got in my head and told me to be quiet, but it was too late. My lie was already burning up my throat. "Mr. O'Leary's telling my daddy so right now."

Miss James x-rayed me with her eyes. I tried to hide my not-truth in the dark part of my tummy, but she saw it anyway.

"Let's go, children," Miss James said. "Emily, walk with me."

We walked. Miss James cleared her throat. "Uhm," she said. She turned her voice down low. "So your brother's autistic?"

I nodded.

"Well," Miss James said, but she didn't go on. Instead, she looked at the wall and sighed. "Here we are at the kindergarten room." She put her smile back on and told everyone to wait while she talked to Mrs. Bell.

Leigh tiptoed over to me. "Where were you this morning?"

I stared down at my shoes. "With my mom. She—"

"Oh. Well, guess what? Last night my dad called."

Miss James came out of Mrs. Bell's room. Leigh straightened up like she hadn't been talking without permission.

"Mrs. Bell would be happy to have you wait in her room, Emily," Miss James said.

I watched everyone else going away as I opened the door. Leigh was talking to Anna. She was probably telling her what she was supposed to be telling me.

I slid sideways into the kindergarten room.

I stayed in the kindergarten room 'til lunch time. I watched the clock, it was past time. But the bell forgot to ring. I watched the second hand go round and round while Mrs. Bell made everyone get their outside things on and line up at the door. My stomach felt tighter than tight. What if Miss James forgot about me? The kindergarten would be closed up and everyone else would be at lunch and I would have to sit outside in the rain.

"Mrs. Bell?" I said, but she was helping someone put on boots and didn't hear me.

Finally footsteps went tap tap tap down the hall. Miss James! I let my breath out slowly as she came in the room.

"Sorry, sorry," Miss James said to Mrs. Bell. "We ran over a little. Come on, Emily."

My feet wanted to run but I told them to be patient. I walked slow and careful like a grown-up. Miss James walked fast, I had to turn the speed up on my legs after all.

Miss James took her keys out too fast and they fell on the floor. "Everyone's at lunch already," she said. "Hurry and get your things so you can join them."

I skated into the classroom on invisible skates. There was a yellow piece of paper on my desk. I read it on the way to my cubby.

Dear Parents,

The Christmas season is fast approaching. It's time to begin teaching our children the value of giving.

We are going to have a grab bag at our Christmas party on Friday, December 23. Please—

"You need to move a little faster," Miss James said.

I put the paper in my coat. "How come we have a Christmas party and not a Chanukah party?"

Miss James looked up from the pile of papers on her desk. "We'll talk about that later. Come on."

I put my coat over my arm, I was a pioneer lady going to the general store. Mr. O'Leary came into the room to talk to Miss James. I almost bumped him on my way out. I stopped in the doorway and put my fingers in my mouth while I listened.

"New development," Mr. O'Leary said. "Emily may be leaving us. So we have to . . ." He twisted his head around. "Go ahead, Emily. No need to wait."

I backed away, watching him.

Joey got up as I walked into the lunchroom. "Hi, Jew," he said. "How are you, Jew?"

"That's not my name." I sat down next to Leigh.

"That's not my name," Joey said in a squeaky voice. He gave me a mean look before he walked away.

Leigh went on eating like nothing happened.

"How was the rehearsal?" I said. I wanted to hear me to make sure I hadn't turned invisible.

"Fine."

I opened up my lunch. "Wanna trade?"

"Nope."

I waited for Leigh to turn around but she didn't. I took my sandwich over to the window and watched the rain fall down.

Leigh slid closer to Anna and whispered something in her ear. Anna giggled.

I pressed my nose against the window, but I could feel them looking at me.

During story time, I felt inside my sock to make sure I didn't lose Uncle Max's key. Leigh turned around and told me to be quiet.

The second hand was going around the clock slower than usual. I stared at Leigh's back instead. It was stiff and angry and I didn't know why.

Miss James looked at me over the top of her book. I turned towards her before she could say, "Eyes forward."

After a long, long time the bell rang.

"Hey, Leigh," I said as we lined up by the door. Leigh didn't turn around. "Leigh," I said again.

Leigh's eyes were on fire. "What?"

I took a step back. "Why are you mad at me?"

"Cause."

"Cause why?"

Leigh crossed herself. "I don't want to be friends with you anymore, OK?" She held her hands over her forehead like they were stuck. "You have the devil in you cause you're Jewish. Joey told me."

I stared Leigh down. She backed away.

Miss James was helping Anna with her coat. I ran up to her. "Miss James. Leigh said—"

"You need to wait, Emily."

I tugged on the bottom of Miss James' coat. She looked up and said in her angry voice, "I said that you need to wait."

"But this is important."

Miss James sighed. "Please go wait by the door."

I didn't go to the door. Instead I put my head down on my desk and listened to everyone getting ready to leave.

After a long time, I heard Miss James tap tap tapping to my desk. "Emily?" she said. "What is it?"

I lifted my head slowly. Miss James said, "The rest of you may leave." Everyone ran out of the room, they pushed and shoved and laughed.

I could feel my eyes crying. I sniffed hard to make them stop. Miss James sat down on top of the desk next to me and smoothed out her skirt.

"Leigh's not my friend anymore." I wiped my eyes with the back of my sleeve. "She said that Joey said I'm the devil cause I'm Jewish."

Miss James turned whiter than the chalk on the board. "Oh dear." She jumped off the desk and ran to the door. "Joey. Leigh."

Miss James came back inside. "They're gone. But I'll talk to them tomorrow. All right?"

I shrugged.

Miss James looked over me and out the window. "How about I walk you out?"

We didn't say anything as we went down the long hall. I stared at my feet the whole way.

Uncle Max was standing right outside the door. "Emily. Finally. Your mom's worrying me to death."

Uncle Max opened his phone. I ran to him and hugged him tight. He closed the phone again and put his hand on top of my head. "What's up?"

I didn't answer. I just squeezed Uncle Max tighter.

"Excuse me," Uncle Max said to Miss James. "What happened?"

Miss James squeezed her hands together. "I probably should be talking to Emily's parents about this . . . I don't . . ."

"Tell me." Uncle Max's voice was messed up by the rain.

Miss James pushed her hair out of her eyes. "How much do you know about Emily's . . . uh, her situation with our Christmas concert?"

"Enough."

"OK. Good." Miss James played with her hood string. "Well, uh, this has gone way beyond what it should have. Please believe me, I tried to stop it. I knew we shouldn't have pulled Emily out of the concert. But my principal wouldn't listen."

Uncle Max squeezed my shoulder so hard it almost hurt. "Yeah, well, he's—" He looked at me. "Never mind that. What's happened now?"

"Uh, there was an incident. Some of the children are, well, they're shunning Emily because she's Jewish."

Uncle Max hugged me so tight I could barely breathe. "I see."

"I'm so sorry." Miss James stared at a puddle on the ground. "This divisiveness is so against the spirit of the season. Things have gone too far and I don't know—"

"Let her sing." Uncle Max's voice was sharp like the edge of a knife. I shivered under his warm hug.

Miss James squeezed her hands so hard the color went out of them. "My principal—"

"Forget him." Uncle Max's eyes flashed fire. "Someone has to make this right." Uncle Max stared Miss James down. Her eyes got wide but she didn't budge.

"I'm so sorry," Miss James said again.

Uncle Max steered me away. I wanted to ask him to carry me but I knew I was too heavy. Instead I leaned on him. The burning in my eyes mixed with the rain falling on me and made my nose run.

Uncle Max's phone rang as he opened his car. He sighed. "Go ahead in."

I got in the front seat while the phone rang again.

"Hey, Bec," Uncle Max said. "I was about to call you, I swear. Yeah, I got her. Relax, will you? She's fine." Uncle Max squeezed the phone tight. "Something happened, Bec. I don't want to talk about it now. I want . . . All right, fine. There was an incident, OK?"

Uncle Max turned the car on. I started to pull on my seatbelt, but he leaned over and did it for me. "Just an incident. No, don't . . . OK, fine, whatever. I know you've got a key. Don't–" He pulled the parking thing so hard I thought it would break. "Right now. Bye."

Uncle Max hit the turn signal thing harder than hard. He breathed deep before he pulled away from the curb.

We were quiet 'til we got to Uncle Max's block. Then I said, "Uncle Max?"

Uncle Max patted my hand. "Everything's gonna be OK." He pressed a button on the ceiling of the car. A gate opened up. The car came forward, I hoped the gate didn't try to eat it.

Uncle Max parked the car. "Well," he said. "Here we are."

I pressed the button to take my seatbelt off. It jumped back like it couldn't wait to be away from me. Maybe it didn't like Jews either.

I squeezed Uncle Max's hand the whole way upstairs like I was Mama squeezing Daddy's hand. Uncle Max took a long time finding his keys. He kept looking at me like he wanted to say something, but he didn't.

Finally, he opened the door. Mama was inside, staring at the TV even though it wasn't on.

"There you are," Mama said. "Thank God. Is Emily OK?"

Uncle Max breathed deep. "Let's get her dried off."

"I'll get her a towel." Mama hurried into the bathroom. She came back with an old blue towel. It tried to scratch me up as I dried myself off.

Uncle Max went into the kitchen.

"Maxwell?" Mama said. "What happened?"

Uncle Max opened a soda can. It didn't like being opened, air hissed from it.

Mama jumped back. "What is that?"

Uncle Max showed her. "Relax, Bec. It's just a Coke." He walked over to the window. "We have enough problems without adding me drinking to the list."

I squinted at the can to see what made it a not-drink, but Mama's eyes interrupted my x-ray. "Are you sure you're all right?"

Uncle Max squeezed the can. "No," he said. "I'm not. And neither is Emily. But at least . . ." He squashed the empty can in his hand. He sighed as it bounced off the trash can. His sigh made him shiver.

I looked at Mama, but she didn't see. She was too busy squeezing the arms of the chair like she was afraid she might fall out.

Uncle Max picked up the can again. "You wanted to know what happened. OK. I was waiting forever. You know that. Then Emily came out with her teacher. She was upset and—"

"Miss James came out? Why? Isn't Emily behaving herself?"

"I'm sure she is. That's got nothing to do—"

"Hey," I said. "Where's Alex?"

Mama turned towards me like she didn't know I was there. "Oh. Daddy's watching him. I'm sorry, Maxwell. What were you saying?"

Uncle Max dropped the can into the trash. "Never mind. Listen, do you have her principal's number?"

"Why?"

Uncle Max looked straight at Mama. "He made a stupid, ignorant decision, and Emily's paying for it. Someone has to straighten him out."

Mama squeezed the arms of the chair so hard I thought they would break off. "Stay out of it, Maxwell."

Uncle Max's eyes flashed. "Who's gonna fix this, then? You? Dan? That coward of a teacher?"

Mama stood up. She was littler than Uncle Max, but she made herself grow until they were the same size. "I mean it. This doesn't concern you."

"Doesn't concern me?" Uncle Max said. "Right. I was there, Rebekah. Emily came out of the building looking like a . . . like some kind of ghost. If you'd seen the way she clung to me . . . I'm sorry, Bec, but I can't stay out of this."

Uncle Max pulled the refrigerator open so hard it moved away from its place on the wall. I jumped back.

"Well, anyway, it doesn't Maxer," Mama said. "We're putting Emily in private school after Christmas."

"Really?"

Mama's eyes sparkled. "Yep. No more Christmas concerts or crazy principals or—"

"Or Anti-Semitic classmates?" Uncle Max said.

Mama's knees trembled. "What?"

"Rebekah. Some of Emily's classmates hate her because she's Jewish." Uncle Max opened a new soda. "Now do you see why this whole mess has to be straightened out?"

Mama stared at the ground.

I dropped to my knees and crawled towards Uncle Max. "I wanna soda."

Mama rocked back and forth. She looked slowly up at Uncle Max. "No, Maxwell. I don't. This makes no difference. Emily's leaving and all of them can go—" She glanced at me. "Well, you know."

I crawled closer. "Soda."

"Get up off the floor, Emily," Mama said. "You're going to get your pants all dirty."

Uncle Max looked at me and Mama like he was taking a picture with his memory. "I guess there's nothing left to say."

"I guess not." Mama squeezed her hands together. "Get up, Emily. We're going now."

Uncle Max held tight to the soda. "Please don't do this," he said. "Look, forget I said anything. Have Dan bring the baby over. I'll make dinner."

Mama looked at Uncle Max. She was wearing her worried face. "No, Maxwell," she said. "Not tonight. Come on, Emily."

"Bec, please. I was only trying to help. Don't—"

"Maxwell. Don't get like this. It's not good for you." Mama reached for my hand. I pulled it away and put it in my pocket where she couldn't get it.

Mama blinked hard, but she turned and walked away like she didn't care.

Uncle Max sank into the chair. I wanted to go to him, but a big clap of thunder told me not to.

"Uncle Max?" I said.

Uncle Max dug around in the chair pocket. “Go with your mom, OK?” He took out his pipe and put it in his mouth.

There was another big clap of thunder. I turned and ran out of the room.

I raced the rain down the steps, but the thunder beat me to the door.

NINE

By dinner the rain was coming down so hard that some men in orange vests came and closed up the street. Mama stood watching them with her nose against the glass. "Street's flooded," she said.

Daddy put some potatoes on a little plate for Alex. "Come sit, Rebekah. Please."

Mama sighed louder than the wind. She came to the table. "I wish this rain would stop."

Daddy didn't answer. He just looked at Mama with his worried face on.

I turned my piece of chicken upside down. "Is the rain gonna make our house float away?"

"Don't worry about it." Daddy said. He mashed a big blob of butter into his potatoes. "So . . . Mama told me that some people at school are not being very nice to you."

I squeezed my fork tight. Daddy's eyes were blue as beach water. I looked away.

"Well?" Daddy's voice was soft but it sounded impatient.

Way over on the other side of the table, the flames were dancing in the menorah. "One, two, three, four, five, six," I said. "Chanukah is almost over."

"Yes. It is." Daddy sighed. "Come on, Emily. You were crying before. Why?"

I watched Mama pick at a loose thread in the tablecloth. "'Cause of Leigh."

"I knew it," Mama said. "I never thought that kid was really Emily's friend."

Daddy held up his hand. "And what did Leigh say that upset you so much?"

Mama pulled the thread so hard it ripped. "Do you have to talk about this during dinner?"

"Yes. We do." Daddy's voice hit Mama hard. She scrunched down like she wished she could melt. "I'm tired of putting everything off," Daddy said in a quieter voice. "Your brother's right. We have to talk about things sometime."

Mama threw her fork down. "Leave Maxwell out of this." She went in the kitchen.

Daddy breathed hard as he watched the kitchen door close. A car outside made a big noise. Alex shrieked.

Daddy got up. "It's all right."

Alex tried to bang his head on the high chair tray but Daddy's hand came out quick and blocked him. He picked up Alex and hugged him tight.

Daddy opened the kitchen door a crack. "Rebekah?"

Mama didn't answer.

Daddy stood still, looking into the kitchen. I slid off my seat and tiptoed behind him so I could see too.

Mama was bent over the sink faucet. She was crying.

I turned away quick and went back to my seat. I still had half a potato, I had to eat it by order of the king or else my head would be chopped off.

Daddy went all the way in the kitchen. "Rebekah, honey, don't." He closed the door with his foot.

I picked up my fork and waited. Mama and Daddy had their voices so low I couldn't hear and Alex had stopped crying. The only sound in the whole house came from the wind blowing against the windows. I wished Alex was here with me.

I shivered and walked over to the menorah to say the candle prayer. In my head I made up words so God would know what I was saying.

Daddy came out of the kitchen. He raised his eyebrows at me as he put Alex back in his chair. I looked away but I went back to my seat.

I stabbed my potato. It bled yellow butter. I shoved it in my mouth anyway so I wouldn't have to talk.

"Stop eating for a minute," Daddy said. "I want to talk to you."

I stared down at my plate. The butter was all over, it looked like a whole lake full. I pushed my potato towards it.

"Look at me, will you?" Daddy said.

I looked up slowly. I was scared of his eyes.

"I am so sorry about what happened to you today, Emily. It's not your fault. It's theirs." Daddy sighed. "I didn't think I'd ever have to talk to you about this. There are people in the world, Emily, who hate us because we're Jewish."

I squirmed. "Miss James says it's not nice to say hate."

"She's right. It's not nice. But it's true."

Mama came out of the kitchen. She dabbed her eyes with a napkin and smiled at us. Her smile looked sad.

Mama walked around the table. She stared into the menorah flame, breathing deep.

She blew the flame out.

"What—" Daddy said.

Mama shoved the menorah away. "What do we need this thing for? It just gets in the way of our lives."

Daddy felt under his shirt for his Jewish chain. "Rebekah."

"Let's eat." Mama poured herself a glass of wine from the bottle in the center of the table. Her hand trembled.

"Let me do that." Daddy grabbed the bottle out of her hand.

Mama drank the wine fast. She put the glass down and gasped like she couldn't breathe.

I stirred my potatoes with my fork. "Daddy?"

"Eat," Daddy said. "Don't play."

The phone rang.

Mama and Daddy looked at each other, but they didn't get up. I pushed my chair back slowly and listened to it ring again. Then I ran into the kitchen.

"Hi, Emily," the voice on the other end of the phone said. "Are you feeling better?"

I looked out at Mama and Daddy. Mama was shoveling food onto her plate and Daddy was staring at the menorah like the flame was still there.

"A little, I guess," I said, and twisted the phone cord.

"Well, we're going to have some talks tomorrow that will help. In the meantime, I need to talk to your mom or dad, OK?"

I dropped the phone and ran into the dining room. "Daddy."

Daddy jerked awake. "Who is it?"

I shrugged.

Daddy sighed as he went to get it. I turned around so I could listen better, but he saw me and closed the door.

I sniffed Mama's empty wine glass. It was sour. "Mama?"

"What is it, baby?"

"Why do people drink this stuff?"

"I don't know." Mama traced the circle on top of the glass. "No reason, really. It just makes you dizzy, so you forget."

"Forget what?"

Mama pushed the glass away. "Come on. While Daddy's on the phone, let's look at your new school on the computer."

I followed Mama into the little room behind her room. She sank into her chair and played with the mouse while the computer came on.

I tiptoed away and got Patrick from my bed. He was sleepy but I made him come to Mama's room with me anyway.

Mama was staring at the screen. Nothing was on yet.

"Mama?" I said.

The computer whirred and put on a screen that said, "Dan loves Rebekah forever."

Mama moved the mouse to make the screen go away. "Uh-huh."

"Will there be a lot of Jewish people at my new school?"

Mama's back got stiff. She swirled the mouse around its pad. "Jewish, not Jewish . . . who cares? There'll be lots of people like you. Now, how do we get on the Internet again?"

I pointed. "Click here, Mama."

"Don't touch the screen. Daddy hates cleaning off fingerprints." Mama typed something into the Internet. I stood on my tiptoes but I couldn't see what it said.

"Mama?"

Mama turned and looked at me.

I took a step back. "Patrick wants to know . . ." I squeezed Patrick tighter than tight. "Is Leigh right?"

Mama moved the mouse. "About what?"

I rubbed the top of Patrick's head. "About Jews and stuff."

Mama grabbed the mouse and clicked hard. Happy music played. "Of course not. Why would you even ask that?"

I looked down at the carpet. It was all ripped up, you could see the floor coming up through it. "You hate Jewish people, Mama."

Mama's hand slipped off the mouse. "Come over here and look at this." She clicked on something. The computer changed its screen to a picture of people sitting on the floor reading books. Everyone was smiling, but their smiles were just camera smiles. They weren't real.

"Look, look," Mama said. "You'll get to read books on your level."

Daddy came upstairs before I could think of something to say. He pushed the door open and came in fast like Superman.

"Oh, there you are." Daddy's breath came out ahead of his words.

"Who was on the phone?" Mama said.

"Emily's teacher. She wants us to come in tomorrow when we drop Emily off."

Mama's hand shook. I looked at Daddy but he didn't see.

"I don't see how there can possibly be school if this rain doesn't stop," Mama said.

Daddy pretended not to hear, but he bit his lip. "What are you guys looking at?" he asked.

"Oh, nothing much."

Daddy looked anyway. "You have your heart set on sending her here, don't you?"

Mama's eyes got big as saucers. "It's a good school, Dan."

"I'm sure it is. But Bec, our finances . . ." Daddy saw me looking up at him. He sighed. "We'll figure it out later."

Patrick made a question mark with his trunk. "What's finances?" I asked. No one answered. I looked at Daddy. "Daddy, what's—"

Daddy's hands fell against his sides like they were too heavy. "Money." He put his hand on Mama's shoulder but she said, "Not in front of Emily."

"Right." Daddy sighed. "Go clear the table, Emily."

I climbed carefully off the bed. "I have to tuck Patrick in first." No one answered. No one even moved.

I hugged Patrick tight and walked away.

The next morning, Mama came downstairs with Alex on her arm like an old rag doll while I was eating breakfast.

"Aren't you coming with us?" I said.

Mama looked at me but all she said was, "I'm leaving now, Dan. Can you help me with Alex's seat?"

"Yeah." Daddy turned towards me. His eyes were shiny. "Emily, I want your cereal bowl empty by the time I get back."

I watched them leave. Mama walked faster than fast. Daddy put his hand on her shoulder to keep her steady, but it fell off again.

I took a bite of my oatmeal. It tasted like sand.

I looked over at the door. Daddy was still outside, talking to Mama. I slid off my seat and tiptoed to the sink. I scraped off the oatmeal and washed it away.

Daddy came inside. "You're even washing your bowl. Wonderful."

"Daddy?"

Daddy turned around, but I had swallowed my conscience. "Never mind."

Daddy breathed in wind and let it out again. "Go get dressed, Emily."

I scrubbed the bowl harder. Daddy came up behind me, his shadow almost knocked me over. I let him take the bowl away.

I backwards-walked out of the kitchen. Then I ran upstairs and slammed my door tight.

It was raining again by the time we got to school. I watched the water dripping down the windshield and took off my seatbelt.

Daddy grabbed my hand too tight. I tried to pull away but it just made him squeeze tighter.

We went in. Mr. O'Leary was coming down the hall. "Dr. Horowitz. What a pleasure."

Daddy took a giant breath and let it out. "Come on, Emily."

Mr. O'Leary nodded hello to me. I lifted my head as high as it would go as we passed him.

The door to Miss James' room was wide open. Something moved by the window. I pushed my head in further so I could see but Daddy shoved me back and fast-walked into the room. I tiptoed in after him.

Miss James was pacing back and forth by the window. She turned on her heel. "Good morning." She stared at the ground. "None of the other parents were able to make it. Nevertheless, we—"

Daddy snapped his coat against the back of a chair. "What are you doing about this situation?"

Miss James lifted her head. "Just because the other parents didn't show up doesn't mean I won't keep trying. In the meantime, I'll talk to the children today." She looked over her shoulder at the clock. "This is so frustrating. I had really hoped that I could get everyone involved together, but clearly that wasn't the case."

An invisible weight fell on Daddy and made his shoulders fall down. "Clearly. If there's nothing else . . ."

"Wait."

Daddy sighed. "What?"

"Emily's been different lately. More quiet. Withdrawn."

"Has she? I hadn't noticed."

"Yes, well." Miss James cleared her throat. "She asked me about autism. She's confused about her brother." She squeezed her hands together. "I think you should talk to her."

Daddy looked at me. He had a scared face on. I slid under a desk to get away from him.

"This must be very difficult," Miss James said.

Daddy's back stiffened. "This," he said, "is none of your business."

"Maybe not. However—"

"No howevers," Daddy said in his no-nonsense voice. He threw his coat across his arm. "Stay out of it. Just resolve this other thing." He started to walk away. I jumped up so fast my head hit the top of the desk.

Daddy turned around. "What are you doing down there, Emily?"

"Watching an ant."

"Get up, please."

I didn't want to but Daddy was looking at me.

"That's better." Daddy bent down so I could kiss his cheek. "Be good."

His footsteps went thump thump thump down the hall.

On the wall, the clock ticked in time with the rain.

I ran to the window and pressed my nose against the glass, but Daddy was long gone.

TEN

Miss James sent me out in the hall while she cleaned up the classroom. The first graders were already running in, they almost knocked me over. Leigh, Joey, and Anna made a tight little knot in the middle of everybody.

Leigh stared at me for a long time. Then she turned her back on me.

Miss James opened the door. "Come in, children." I tried to put magic on Leigh as she passed so she would be my friend again.

Joey knocked into me. "Quit blocking the road."

I watched my feet as I walked in. I put one foot in front of the other like I was a tightrope walker.

Miss James had moved the desk around to make a circle and put our nametags on them so we would know where to sit. She walked behind the circle. I ducked as she passed me.

Leigh raised her hand. "Miss James! Why are the desks—"

Miss James crossed her arms. "We'll talk about that after the pledge."

I watched everybody stand up one by one. We sounded like robot soldiers as we did the Pledge of Allegiance.

I looked at Leigh. She was staring straight ahead like she was trying to turn off her eyes. Her chest was puffed full of breath.

"Leigh." Miss James bent her music book back so it would stay open. "Switch with Anna, please."

Leigh crossed herself. "Move."

Miss James came into the middle of the circle and looked around. I sat up straighter than straight when her eyes landed on me.

"I want to talk to you all," Miss James said, "about something that happened yesterday afternoon."

Joey was rolling his pencil down the desk, over and over. Miss James grabbed it away. "Someone in this class told someone else that they could not be friends because they were different religions."

I slid down in my seat in case anyone guessed Miss James was talking about me.

"This makes me sad, boys and girls. First of all, it isn't true. Anyone can be friends with anybody. What, Joey?"

Joey squirmed in his seat. "This is music time, not talking time. Let's go."

Miss James made her jaw tight. "We are not having music time this morning."

Miss James stared Joey down. He looked away first.

"You want to know what it feels like?" Miss James said. She counted off groups of three. "Get the math work done. No talking to anyone not in your group. See how far you get."

Miss James turned her back on us. I looked at Leigh, she looked away. I sighed and picked up my pencil.

Miss James came over. She bent down and whispered, "Emily. Go in the middle of the circle."

I jumped up so fast my chair fell back, but I remembered to walk slow. There were four chairs in the middle of the circle. I sat in one of them and watched Miss James getting Leigh and Joey.

When we were all in the circle, Miss James said, "Now." She looked at the three of us like she didn't know what to do next. "Let's talk about yesterday. Joey—"

The door opened. Its shadow cut off Miss James' sentence.

Mr. O'Leary stomped in like the giant in *Jack and the Beanstalk*.

"Hello, Mr. O'Leary," Miss James said. She turned back around. "Did you tell Leigh that Jews are the devil?"

"Interesting lesson." Mr. O'Leary walked around the circle. "However, the children should be in the auditorium right now."

"I realize that," Miss James said. "But—"

"I'll see you in five minutes."

Miss James watched Mr. O'Leary's back going towards the door. "Mr. O'Leary?"

Mr. O'Leary turned around. "Is there a problem?"

"Well, uh, there is a situation that you should be aware of."

"Oh?"

"Some of the children have, well, they've been picking on Emily because of . . ." Miss James turned into a girl littler than me. She stared at the floor. "Because of her Jewish heritage."

"I see." Mr. O'Leary played with a button on the end of his sleeve. "Well, I'm sure it's nothing you can't handle." He started to walk away. "Four minutes, Miss James."

Miss James didn't turn around until Mr. O'Leary was all the way gone. When she did, her lips were tighter than tight and her face was pink. She clapped her hands. "Line up, children."

I stared at my feet.

"Emily," Miss James said. "Come lead the line."

I shuffled all the way to the front of the room. "Forward march." I took robot soldier steps to Mrs. Bell's room.

"Keep going," Miss James said. I looked at her. Her eyes were full of light but it wasn't the good kind, they looked the way Mama's do when she's about to turn mean. I folded myself up and shuffled away.

Mr. O'Leary was sitting in the front row when we got to the music room. I put two fingers in my mouth and watched him.

Everyone started shoving and running. "Come on, Emily." Miss James said.

I took baby robot steps.

"All the way. And take your fingers out of your mouth, please." Miss James turned towards the risers. "Anna, move over a little. We need room for Emily."

Anna looked over her shoulder at Leigh, but she scooted over. I stared at them.

"We're waiting, Emily," Miss James said.

The riser creaked when I stepped on it like it was going to open up and make me fall through.

Mr. O'Leary cleared his throat. Miss James sat down at the piano anyway.

Mr. O'Leary came over to her. "Miss James."

"Just a moment." Miss James squinted at the music even though she had her glasses on.

Mr. O'Leary stared at me 'til I looked at the floor. "I hope she apologized," he said to Miss James.

Miss James stopped playing. She lifted her head slowly and stared at Mr. O'Leary. "Of course."

Mr. O'Leary's head made a popping noise as he turned around. He rubbed the back of his neck. "Emily," he said. "I am really looking forward to hearing you sing."

Mr. O'Leary x-rayed me. I held tight to myself so I wouldn't melt away.

Miss James' shoulders shook. "All right, children. Let's show Mr. O'Leary how beautifully we can sing."

I squeezed my eyes shut. *Please don't be mad, God. If I don't sing, Miss James will get in trouble . . .*

I opened my eyes slowly and lifted my head up so it was out of Mr. O'Leary's reach.

Miss James pointed to us. I kept my voice quiet as I sang and I skipped the word "Jesus," just in case.

When the song ended, Mr. O'Leary looked straight at me and said, "Thank you, children." He turned and walked away.

"Well," Miss James said. "I think we can see that Emily is not trying to ruin our concert, can't we?"

I didn't dare look at Joey as I climbed slowly off the risers. My cheeks felt tight. I bent down and pretended to tie my shoe so I wouldn't get sick again.

The bell rang. The ringing got stuck in my head and made me dizzy.

When we got back to our room, Miss James said, "I think I've made my point. Let's have our social studies lesson." She sat down at her desk. "If everyone would turn to page thirty-seven—"

My cheeks felt tighter than tight. I waved my hand back and forth like a flag.

Miss James turned her eyes away. "Let's look at the discussion questions, shall we?"

I jumped up. "Miss James."

Miss James looked at me. "That behavior's not appropriate, Emily."

I felt dizzy again, but my legs would not let me sit down. I grabbed onto the desk and squeezed hard. Leigh and Anna and Joey giggled. I thought hard about something else until my brain felt like it was breaking in half.

Miss James got up from her desk. "Quiet, children." Her voice echoed and made my head hurt. "Emily? What's the Maxer?"

My mouth opened and closed but nothing came out. I was turning into a fish. I breathed hard. "I don't feel good." A tear came out of my eye even though I told it to stay put.

"Cry baby. Cry baby," Joey said, and one by one everyone repeated it.

"I said be quiet," Miss James said. "Leigh, walk Emily to the nurse's office, please."

Leigh started to cross herself but Miss James was looking so she stopped.

"Now, Leigh," Miss James said in a Mama voice.

Leigh got up. "Come on," she said, but she didn't give me her hand. I started to give her mine, but she was already leaving. I looked at my feet so I could keep the throw-up down until I was in the nurse's office.

When we got there, Leigh told Mrs. Goshen I was sick and started to walk away.

Mrs. Goshen got up from behind her desk. "Wait a minute." She breathed hard as she came forward. "What's wrong with her?"

Leigh shrugged.

My legs felt like they were turning into rubber bands. I grabbed onto the nurse's desk.

Mrs. Goshen looked over at me. "She's dizzy? Fine. Good. You may go."

Leigh watched Mrs. Goshen put a thermometer strip around my forehead. After a long time, she flipped her hair over her shoulder and walked away.

Mrs. Goshen clicked her tongue on her teeth while she looked at the thermometer strip. I tried to see but my head hurt too much.

"Fever, dizziness," Mrs. Goshen said. "Want to go home?"

I nodded. I was afraid to open my mouth. I was sweating so hard I wished I could change into pajamas.

The bell rang.

Everyone else was going to lunch.

ELEVEN

It was quiet downstairs when I woke up the next morning. I pulled my socks up high to keep me warm and tiptoed into the kitchen.

Mama and Daddy were at the table, holding hands. "Are you hungry?" Mama asked.

I rubbed my stomach to ask it if I could eat. "Maybe a little."

"Sit down," Daddy said. He was gruff as the Big Bad Wolf. "Mama and I have something to tell you."

The phone rang.

Mama froze in the middle of putting jelly on toast.

"Well," Daddy said, "remember when we talked about finances?" The phone rang again and again. "Rebekah. Could you please get that?"

Mama slammed the knife down. "You know, I can't do everything." She picked up the phone so hard it almost came out of the wall. "Yes?" She twisted the phone cord around her fingers. "Maxwell. How much did you drink?"

I picked up Daddy's glass and stared into it. Daddy got up to get me some juice, but I shook my head.

"Please don't . . ." Mama bit her lip. "Fine."

Mama slammed the phone down. She turned around slowly. "Maxwell," she said, "is on his way over."

I wanted to cheer but I was too scared. Instead I held tight to the table and waited for my head to stop feeling dizzy.

"Is he?" Daddy said.

Mama looked at me. "Get Emily upstairs. I don't want—"

"What about my toast?" I said.

Mama pinched the space at the top of her nose. "Dan, please . . ."

"Come on." Daddy gave me his hand. I squeezed my chair tight but he said, "Now."

When we got to my room, my brain was throbbing. Daddy watched me grab onto the bed to get in it. His eyes looked gray and empty.

I wrapped the covers around me to keep the cold out. Daddy sat down on the edge of the bed and tapped me on my legs. I pulled them in. "I'm not a drum."

"Sorry." Daddy put his chin in his hands. "Listen to me, Emily. You're not the only one who's sick. Uncle Max—"

I grabbed Patrick. "He's OK, isn't he?"

"He'll be fine." Daddy sighed. "It's hard to explain. He's just not himself today. Stay upstairs while he's here. Please."

Patrick pulled his tusks in and got ready to roar, but the doorbell rang. Daddy patted me on the shoulder and walked away like he was on the airport moving belt.

I rolled over and pressed my face into the pillow.

Mama's footsteps came up so hard I felt them in my stomach. "Emily. Leigh's here with your homework."

I closed my eyes and pretended to be a dead person. Mama's footsteps went away.

"Um," Leigh said. I could feel her coming towards me.

"You're taking up my air," I said.

Leigh sat on the bed anyway. "Wanna know a secret?"

I pretended not to hear.

Leigh sighed deep. She sounded like an old lady. "My dad can't come for Christmas. He's giving me a grown-up bike instead." Leigh's voice trembled and made my eyes burn. Patrick told me it was a trap, but I couldn't help it. I sat up.

"Here," Leigh said. She gave me some crumpled up papers. I grabbed them and smoothed them out.

Downstairs, someone opened the door and closed it again. I opened my ears all the way up but the grown-ups went in the kitchen so I couldn't hear.

Leigh stood up. She stared at me like she was waiting for the bell to ring so she could go home. "I'm sorry, Emily."

Mama said a bad word very loud.

Leigh started to cross herself but she saw me looking and backed away. "Stop staring."

"Why?"

Leigh turned her back on me, but her arms were moving so I knew what she was doing. I looked up at the ceiling in case God was there. A white shadow slid across the place where Daddy painted it last year. I looked down again.

A herd of elephants came running up the stairs.

Leigh flinched. "What's that?"

I shrugged. I didn't want Leigh to know about Mama's elephant steps.

Someone grabbed the door and opened it really hard. It flew back and hit the wall. Leigh crouched down by the side of my bed and crossed herself again.

"Hey kiddo," Uncle Max said. The volume thing on his voice was broken, he was way too loud. "I heard you're not feeling well so I decided to check on you."

Mama did a flying leap into the room. Her eyes were big and wide and they glittered with fire. "Get the hell out of here."

Uncle Max rolled his eyes. "Your mom's not too happy with me right now." His words slid into each other and hurt themselves. "She thinks I've been drinking."

Uncle Max leaned towards me. His breath smelled sour. "Just between you and me, I have."

Leigh whimpered. "Joey's right."

I jumped up. My head was dizzy but I didn't care. "Take that back."

Leigh crossed herself again. She backed away from me and Uncle Max. "The devil's here," she whispered.

Uncle Max's eyes flashed fire. "You hear that, Bec?" His voice was still too loud. It made me shiver. "We're devils. We're all devils." He laughed. Even his laugh was broken. "That's why bad things happen to us. We're devils."

"Stop it, Maxwell." Mama's voice was quiet like Uncle Max had taken away all her volume.

"We're devils," Uncle Max said, and laughed again. "Listen . No, you won't. You never do. I can't help it. I have to tell the truth."

Uncle Max came closer to Mama. She ducked away. "The other kids are tor—torturing Emily 'til she's sick and what are you doing about it? I'll tell you what. Nothing. You don't ever do anything for her. You don't really love her. Not like Alex. I mean, you'll waste thousands of dollars and hundreds of hours trying to make him normal instead of lov—loving him the way he is, but—"

Mama's face turned redder than red. She moved towards Uncle Max like a tiger hunting for prey. "I said stop."

Uncle Max's shoulders fell down too far like they didn't know where they were supposed to go. "Whatever. I didn't come here to talk to you anyway. I wanted to talk to Emily. She's sick, you know. And on top of that, she has to stay in public school. You don't have the money. You wasted it on Alex."

The world turned too fast all of a sudden. I grabbed onto the bedpost so I wouldn't fall down.

Leigh looked up from her hands. "You're staying in our class?"

I shrugged.

"What, you haven't told her?" Uncle Max said. Mama jumped away from him. "Of course not. You wouldn't tell her. All you ever do is lie, lie, lie." Uncle Max turned towards me. He wobbled like a jack-in-the-box. "You're not going to private school, kiddo. You can forget it. It's over."

The room spinned faster than fast, it was worse than when the teacup ride made me throw up. "Mama . . . ," I said.

Mama's eyes got wide. There wasn't fire in them now, they were just gray ashes. "Maxwell, please. You're scaring her. Let me take you home."

"I'm scaring her. Right. Fine. OK. I'm scaring her. I get it. You don't want me here. I'm gone. Bye."

Mama watched him go. "Maxwell . . ."

Uncle Max's knees swayed like he was going to fall down. He grabbed onto the door. I looked at Mama and at Leigh, but no one else's eyes saw. Only mine.

Uncle Max held tight to the door. "What do you want from me?"

"Call me tomorrow?" Mama said.

Uncle Max shrugged and walked away. Mama's eyes got big as the moon, she looked at the door. Her magic didn't work. It didn't make Uncle Max come back.

It was snowing in the jungle. I was trying to ride a lion but he wouldn't move. I jumped off, all of a sudden I was in school but Miss James wasn't the teacher now. Alex was.

A train went by and clattered loud while Alex walked around the room. I opened my math workbook so he could see I did everything I was supposed to. He was at Leigh's desk slapping a ruler in his hand and it made me afraid.

The train clattered louder. I looked out the window and wished I was on it.

Alex came to my desk while I wasn't paying attention. He hit himself with the ruler and said something but I couldn't hear him. He was standing so close there was no air left. I gasped for breath. My heart beat fast, fast, fast 'til I thought it would explode.

I opened my eyes and lay flat in bed. Downstairs, Mama was washing the dishes and putting them away. The noise made big cuts in the darkness.

I opened my mouth wide to catch as much air as I could before I went down. My head was not dizzy anymore but I held onto the edges of all the furnitures anyway, I was a baby learning to walk.

When I got into the dining room, Mama was coming towards the menorah with a silver lighter in her hand. I ducked back into the corner. The dark went around me like a blanket and hid me.

Mama lit the top candle. She whispered the Hebrew very fast. Then she pulled the candle up out of its throne. Her hands were shaking so bad I thought she would drop it.

I counted all eight candles in my head as Mama lit them. She put the top candle back slowly and backwards-walked to the wall.

"Forgive me, God," Mama said. "Forgive me, forgive me, forgive me." She hid her head in her hands and cried.

I crawled out of the corner. "What's wrong, Mama?"

Mama flinched. She put her smile on. "Nothing. We forgot to do candles tonight, that's all."

My heart beat a fast happy beat. "Can I help?"

Mama smoothed her pants. "Come in the other room with me. I'll tell you a story."

I followed Mama into the living room. It was way dark, Mama turned into a shadow-Mama and sat down on a shadow couch. I waited for her to say something but she didn't. Instead she stared into space 'til I could barely see her head.

I looked over my shoulder. The flame was still in the menorah where it belonged. "What story?"

"Oh. The . . . the story of Chanukah." Mama patted her lap. "Come here."

Mama tried to put on her smile but it fell off again. I climbed up on the couch next to her.

"The story of Chanukah takes place a long time ago," Mama said. "You see, in those days, there were people who didn't like Jews."

Mama's throat made a crying sound. She sniffed hard. "Oh, Emily. I'm so sorry we can't send you to private school. I . . . I wanted to . . . I still want to . . . but Alex's school is so expensive . . . and Daddy said he needs it more." Mama blinked hard but her tears didn't listen to her eyes, they came out anyway. She hid her head in her hands so I wouldn't see.

I looked at the floor. "Don't be sad, Mama."

Mama pulled her head up slowly like the string on it was broken. "I'm not sad." She smiled, but I knew she was lying. "It's late. Let's go back to bed."

I rubbed my eyes but they wouldn't turn sleepy. "What about the story?"

"Tomorrow, OK?" Mama went fast towards the steps.

My legs didn't want to get up. I traced a circle in the cushion with my finger.

Mama was almost out of the room, but she turned around. "Emily?"

I looked up.

Mama smiled. Her smile was almost real. "I love you."

I sat on the couch for a long time. Then I went to the dining room and looked at the menorah. The flames were standing straight and tall, they were melting the candles away.

Mama came back down. She stood still like a ghost and watched the candles too. After a minute, she tiptoed away again.

The flames danced on top of the candles. I blew them out one by one.

Lightning flashed once, then went away. I waited for a long time, but I never heard thunder.

The rain went tap tap tap against the window.

It was here to wash away the snow.

Turn the page for an excerpt from Stephanie Silberstein's emotional second novel,
CHASING GHOSTS.

Spanning over 20 years of a young woman's life, ***CHASING GHOSTS*** *grapples with the issue of love—young and old—and addresses the question of whether we really ever get over our first love.*

PROLOGUE

Sandra Livingston stared herself down in the mirror. *You are not pregnant.* She put her hand over her stomach while she read the back of the EPT box. She said Paul's name aloud without meaning to.

Sandra tilted her head towards the ceiling. The bulb flickered but it didn't go out. She rubbed the back of her neck while she prayed.

Linda tapped on the door. Sandra pulled her head down. Her neck cracked.

"Mama?" Linda said.

"Just a second, honey." Sandra leaned into the mirror. Her eyes looked less green than they used to and her hair hung in a limp, tangled mess.

She looked old.

Sandra ran her fingers through her hair to pull out the knots.

Paul sank into the bed, that other time, when Sandra told him. She squeezed his hand. He squeezed back real tight, like he was drowning and needed her to pull him up. "Wow," he said.

"Yeah. Wow." Sandra put her free hand over her stomach. "So what do we do?"

Paul didn't answer. He tapped a perfect beat on the floor while he stared into space. It vibrated through Sandra until she felt sick.

"Well?" she said.

Paul dropped Sandra's hand. "I told you it was better for us to just stay friends. Now do you see–"

"Yeah, well, too late now."

"Maybe, maybe not." Paul went over the window. He had his back to Sandra. She knew he was smoking a cigarette. She put her hand over her stomach while she waited for him.

Paul dumped ash into the tray. His shoulders rose and fell. “I only see one solution,” he said.

Sandra dropped her hand. She stared down at her stomach. “You mean . . .”

Paul played with his lighter. “There’s nothing else we can do.”

Now Sandra squeezed her eyes shut to keep the tears in and the memory out. Her ears buzzed. She was dizzy. She grabbed onto the sink until her legs felt like they could hold her again.

Linda banged on the door. “Mama. Let me in before I pee on the floor.”

Sandra jerked awake. “Coming, coming.” She shoved the pregnancy test deep into the spare toilet paper before opening the door.

Linda slid into the bathroom. She stopped right in front of Sandra and hopped on one foot. Sandra stepped back and Linda ducked around her to the toilet. Linda stuck her little nose up and pushed her chin forward. She looked just like Paul.

“Go away,” Linda said.

“Sorry.” The cabinet under the sink was slightly open; Sandra kicked it shut. “You sure you don’t need any help?”

“Mama! “

Sandra heard the cabinet door creaking open again as she walked slowly out of the room. She sat down on the hamper halfway between the bathroom and her childhood bedroom, Linda’s room now. She remembered being a little girl, staring up at a ceiling full of glow-in-the-dark stars. Back then, she put herself to sleep dreaming of visiting those stars. How the hell did she end up 24 years old, alone, with a five-year-old and a bunch of memories?

Sandra put her hand over her stomach again and kicked at the hamper bottom.

Linda came out of the bathroom. “All done, Mama.” She scrunched up her little nose. “What’s wrong?”

Sandra breathed so deep she could taste the air. It was cold and empty. “Nothing. I was just thinking, that’s all.”

Linda wrinkled her brow and hopped on one foot. “Wanna come play Legos with me?”

Sandra made herself smile. “I’ll be there when I get out of the bathroom.”

“’K.” Linda ran down the hall.

Sandra sat for a little while longer, cupping her hands round her stomach. She could feel a squirrel climbing a tree outside. She turned her head and watched orange leaves fall.

Sandra let her breath out slowly. The squirrel climbed halfway down the tree and jumped to the ground.

Sandra checked the bathroom lock twice before she took the pregnancy test.